355.0217

5-50

10097

FIRE FROM THE ASHES

Short stories about Hiroshima and Nagasaki

Edited by
Kenzaburō Ōe

readers international

Jacket painting by Iri & Toshi Maruki
"Mother and Child (part)"
The Hiroshima Panels (xi)

Under the shattered structures
Amidst the excruciating flames
Parent left child, husband left wife,
wife left husband
Escape!

Nowhere to escape to
Fleeing in all directions
Figures running from the terror of the
Bomb

Mothers shielding their babies
from death, dying themselves,
There were oh! so many

This book is based on selections from *Nan to mo Shirenai Mirai ni*,
edited by Kenzaburō Ōe and published in Japan by Shueisha in 1983.
Copyright © 1985 by Shueisha Press. All rights reserved.
Published in association with Readers International,
whose UK editorial branch is at
8 Strathray Gardens, London NW3 4NY, Great Britain.
US Subscriber Service Department: P.O. Box 959, Columbia,
Louisiana 71418 USA.

ISBN 0–930523–09–1 hardcover
ISBN 0–930523–10–5 softcover

The planning of this anthology is one of the activities of the Japan P.E.N. Center.

CONTENTS

Kenzaburō Ōe

Introduction :
Toward the Unknowable Future

THE massive wreckage of life, limb, and livelihood caused by
the atomic bombings of Hiroshima and Nagasaki was, for
single-bomb attacks, unprecedented in human history. In
trying to comprehend this extensive damage in the aftermath
of the Pacific War, the Japanese faced many uncertainties and
ambiguities. Efforts to reach an accurate understanding of this
problem, which concerns all humanity in the latter half of the
twentieth century, have been made by a wide range of citizens'
organizations in which A-bomb survivors themselves have
taken a central role. Literary works dealing with the atomic
bombings have also wrestled with this crucial problem.

Literary treatments of A-bomb damage and suffering have
not all focused solely on the "victim" approach to interpreting
the bombings. The "second-generation survivors" (children of
those directly affected) were the first to acknowledge clearly
that Japan and the Japanese were aggressors in the Pacific War
that brought on the atomic bombings and, before that, in
Japan's war on China. Thus, they sought to comprehend the
atomic bombings in relation to what the Japanese call the
"Fifteen-years War" (1931-45). The second generation's views
found common ground in the A-bomb survivors' organizations to which their fathers and mothers belonged. From this
common ground emerged the core ideas and values by which

they not only question both the American and Japanese governments' responsibilities for the atomic bombings but also have repeatedly urged the Japanese government to take international initiatives to abolish all nuclear arms.

With this broad perspective, the movement has embraced the concerns of various non-Japanese persons, particularly the large numbers of Koreans who were in Hiroshima and Nagasaki in August 1945 and also suffered atomic death, injury, and damage—thus challenging the widespread trend of referring to Japan as "the only country to suffer atomic bombings." The movement has since expanded to join Pacific-area peoples in protests against nuclear contamination of the Pacific Ocean by aggressor nations, including Japan (for nuclear waste dumping). This understanding, rooted in the Japanese experiences of Hiroshima and Nagasaki, is the cornerstone of the growing global antinuclear movement that seeks the eradication of all nuclear arms.

Most literature that has taken A-bomb experiences as its basic subject matter has attempted to see the experiences of Hiroshima and Nagasaki A-bomb survivors as a vital factor in the lives and livelihood of all the Japanese people. The English translation of this anthology of A-bomb short stories is an effort to make the original A-bomb experiences a part of the shared experience of peoples throughout the world.

Among intellectuals who experienced the atomic bombing of Hiroshima and subsequently wrestled with the questions of how to live and how to express themselves as writers, the most outstanding is Tamiki Hara (1905–51). A master of poetic prose suffused with gentleness, Hara experienced the Hiroshima bombing because he had returned there, his hometown, to place in his family's ancestral tomb the ashes of his recently deceased wife. He resolved to give expression, as an eyewitness, to the wretchedness of A-bomb suffering and damage, which he himself had experienced. Beginning with *Natsu no Hana*

(Summer Flower), he persistently resisted censorship restrictions of the Allied Occupation and published many works. Five years later, however, during the Korean War, when it was rumored that atomic bombs might again be used, he committed suicide. The work he left behind at that time, *Shingan no Kuni* (The Land of Heart's Desire), is filled with profound insights for us who must continue living in the nuclear age. Machine-centered civilization, having introduced nuclear devastation, then pushed forward madly along a course of development fueled by nuclear energy. Toward this vigorous pursuit—that could lead to global annihilation and, in any case, faces an "unknowable future"—Hara harbored profound misgivings.

Writer Yōko Ōta (1906–63) had already produced a number of literary works before experiencing the Hiroshima bombing; but she subsequently concentrated all of her energies on writing about A-bomb experiences. While, unlike Hara, she did not succumb to suicide, her untimely death is doubtless evidence that the intense physical and mental anguish she suffered over survivors' A-bomb injuries and illnesses exhausted her strength prematurely. She riveted her sight on human beings at the time of the bombing; her works *Ningen Ranru* (Human Shabbiness) and *Han-ningen* (Half-human) are fruits of her perceptive powers. Viewing the survivors' pains and problems in terms of relations between self and others, she penned a stinging indictment of discrimination against A-bomb survivors. She was particularly gifted at depicting life in Hiroshima in the immediate post-bombing days—the Nagasaki situation was essentially the same—as the survivors struggled amidst a multitude of hardships to rebuild their lives.

Masuji Ibuse (1898–   ), a major representative of modern Japanese literature, did not personally experience the atomic bombings. But, in addition to his award-winning *Kuroi Ame* (Black Rain), he wrote a number of superb short stories about

Hiroshima survivors in the context of the local culture and customs he knew so well (he grew up in a town near Hiroshima). In *Kakitsubata* (The Crazy Iris), Ibuse portrays the misery caused by the atomic bombing; but he does so from the vantage point of daily life in the provincial setting of wartime Japan. The result is a penetratingly accurate portrayal of A-bomb survivors. By focusing on the abnormality of an iris blooming unseasonally, out of step with nature's cycles, and then on the abnormality of "man's inhumanity to man" in the use of atomic weapons and the consequent misery, Ibuse pinpoints at one stroke the views of nature and of life and death involved. Ibuse is surely the best example of literary excellence achieved by writers who throughout a lifetime have dared to face squarely the extraordinary agonies of atomic warfare.

Another outstanding representative of modern Japanese literature and one who, like Ibuse, did not personally experience the atomic bombing of her city, is Ineko Sata (1904–   ). A native of Nagasaki, she has over the years cultivated close relationships with Nagasaki survivors, and she drew on her cumulative insights to produce the full-length novel *Juei* (Shadow of a Tree), which treats the long-term hardships of A-bomb survivors. In the short story *Iro no Nai E* (The Color-less Paintings) she depicts the inner processes—reflected in the colorless paintings—of an A-bomb survivor-painter who, as time passes, sinks into deep depression. Another impressive human dimension of this story is the inclusion of the painter's refusal, as an A-bomb survivor, to participate in a highly politicized world rally against atomic and hydrogen bombs, along with the painter's warm feelings toward the writer herself. World rallies against atomic and hydrogen bombs, held alternatively each year in Hiroshima and Nagasaki on their respective memorial bombing days, with many foreign participants, constitute an important political movement to abolish nuclear arms. Further social significance is added by wide citizen participation in these rallies. Writer Sata, an active leader in progressive women's movements, has played a key role in these world rallies. That she manifests concern for, but without criticizing, A-bomb survivors who turn their backs on overly politicized rallies, reveals Sata's distinctive character.

Hiroko Takenishi (1929–   ), Sata's junior by a quarter of a century, is a writer best known for her studies of classical Japanese literature. She personally experienced the Hiroshima bombing, but she has not resorted to strident expressions to voice her political opinions relative to that experience. Her short story *Gishiki* (The Rite) depicts the inner thought processes of a woman who, having experienced the Hiroshima bombing as a young girl, becomes a mature and independent intellectual; a love affair, however, arouses in her anxiety about possible abnormal genetic effects induced by A-bomb illness, and this leads to various misgivings about marriage and childbirth. This depiction of A-bomb experiences as seen by a woman of intellectual bent who pursues a career in business may well convey to the larger world a new image of women in Japan. Also of special interest is the depiction in bold relief—through the main character's observations as a young girl—of the circumstances of a family of Korean residents in Japan who experienced the atomic bombing.

Another writer who experienced the atomic bombing as a young girl—in her case, in Nagasaki—and has since written various works about that experience is Kyōko Hayashi (1930–   ). She possesses unusual powers of imagination for recalling past experiences with great fidelity and for reconstructing them in detail. And for her, the most significant of all past experiences is that of suffering the atomic bombing as a young girl. Central in her memory are her classmates, both those who were killed instantly by the bombing and those who later died, one after another, from A-bomb injuries and illnesses. The grown, middle-aged woman realizes that, though still living, neither she nor the rest of her classmates are physically or mentally free from the dark shadow cast by the first atomic bombs. *Akikan* (The Empty Can) is one of her many short stories that weave current thoughts and feelings into a portrayal of the cruel events of August 1945. A young girl named Kinuko, not knowing what to do with the remains of her parents who died in the atomic bombing, places their ashes in an empty can, which she then carries with her to school. This past happening is depicted in the manner of a mythical episode. Then, under Hayashi's deft pen, this young girl becomes a grown woman who has all along lived with glass fragments, sprayed widely by the atomic blast, still imbedded in her back; tomorrow, it seems, she will enter a hospital for treatment after thirty long years. Hayashi skillfully connects past and present in this story about a young woman who survives an atomic bombing and goes on living.

Though not himself an A-bomb victim, Mitsuharu Inoue (1926–   ) has also written extensively about Nagasaki A-bomb survivors, focusing especially on the discrimination they suffer in provincial communities. His piercing social sensitivity, first manifested in his full-length novel *Chi no Mure* (People of the Land), comes through also in his short story *Te no Ie* (The House of Hands). This tale involves A-bomb orphans of Nagasaki who are raised in an institution that teaches them manual skills. When they reach marriageable age, one of them, a girl, develops symptoms of A-bomb disease and has a difficult childbirth. By treating fears of radiation aftereffects, a new dimension of social discrimination against survivors is exposed in this story's depiction of a dark crisis. In a postscript to this short story, Inoue presents thought-provoking correlations between discrimination against A-bomb survivors and the historically older, though still active, discrimination against members of outcast communities (*buraku*) in Japan.

The authors thus far introduced, both the A-bomb survivors and those who are not, are all professional writers whose works represent the high quality of Japanese literature. There are, however, many A-bomb survivors of both the Hiroshima and the Nagasaki bombings who have thought through their experiences and, while not professional writers, have expressed themselves in novels and short stories. Choosing to make their primary contributions to society through other occupational channels, they have nonetheless produced many literary works. As a whole, their stories based on A-bomb experiences possess two distinctive characteristics. One is that their way of portraying A-bomb experiences relies on a method of stark realism. Their sometimes artless realism is extremely powerful; and, indeed, their works force one to reconsider the very nature and purpose of a novel. The other point is that almost all of these nonprofessional writers experienced the atomic bombings in their late childhood or early adolescence. They retained vivid memories of their experiences until they reached mature adulthood, when they then performed the valuable service to society of writing stories based on their experiences. *Ningen no Hai* (Human Ashes) by Katsuzō Oda (1931–   ) is included in this volume as representative of works by these writers.

In compiling this anthology I have come to realize anew that the short stories included herein are not merely literary expressions, composed by looking back at the past, of what happened at Hiroshima and Nagasaki in the summer of 1945. They are also highly significant vehicles for thinking about the contemporary world over which hangs the awesome threat of vastly expanded nuclear arsenals. They are, that is, a means for stirring our imaginative powers to consider the fundamental conditions of human existence; they are relevant to the present and to our movement toward all tomorrows. As I noted at the outset, in the work he left behind before committing suicide, Hara Tamiki warned that, because civilization is headed either toward extinction or toward salvation from that fate, we inescapably face an "unknowable future." The fundamental condition of life, then, is that we are assailed by overwhelming fear yet, at the same time, beckoned by the necessity to rebuild hope, however difficult, in defiance of that fear. These are the basic issues that underlie the short stories presented in this anthology.

translated by David L. Swain

Masuji Ibuse

The Crazy Iris

SHORTLY after Hiroshima was bombed, I was at a friend's house in the outskirts of Fukuyama looking at an iris which had flowered out of season. It grew alone and its blossoms were purple.

This was in the middle of August, some days after the Imperial Rescript of Surrender. Most of the irises were clustered at one end of the pond and already displayed their long, tonsured, bright green pistils. But this belated plant grew somewhat apart from the others; out of its sharp leaves, which rose from the water, emerged a delicate stem and at the end of this, the twisted, purple blossoms. When first I caught sight of it from the window of my friend's house, I thought it was a piece of colored tissue paper floating on the pond . . . .

It is a hundred miles from Fukuyama to Hiroshima. At about noon on the day Hiroshima was bombed, I went for a walk through Fukuyama. Several of the shops were advertising bargain sales. On display was a motley collection of antique household articles at absurdly low prices: chests of drawers, desks, mirror-stands, a ping-pong table, tableware, an antler, a bearskin. Outside the shutters of one shop were hung dozens of large mats with a sign, "These mats for sale. Thirty sen each." A huge Imari-ware flowerpot, tightly planted with palm-bamboos, bore the notice, "These palm-bamboos for sale. Price including pot: Eighty sen." A small organ was selling for five yen. A vase with a red plant was ten sen; three bamboo clothes-poles came to fifteen sen; a history of Japan in fourteen volumes was fourteen yen.

"Hey, Masu, what are you up to?" I heard a voice behind me. "You weren't going to pass without stopping to see me!" It was the proprietor of the Yasuhara Pharmacy standing at the entrance of his shop in a white cotton shirt, hammer in hand. Mr. Yasuhara and I came from the same village, some seven miles outside Fukuyama, and we had been brought up together as children. He had moved to this town some twenty years before and now ran a large, well-stocked pharmacy.

We stood chatting in front of the shop.

"I'm having my last look at it all," I said. "I don't suppose there'll be much left after the bombers have been here. You've seen those handbills the Americans dropped, haven't you? I suppose you'll be leaving here?"

"Yes, now that they've issued the evacuation order, I'll be clearing out as soon as I can get things into shape. But you know, Masu, they can't expect me to do it all in a few minutes."

Mr. Yasuhara turned towards his shop and continued nailing a wooden board to the door. According to the evacuation order, all householders were to board up their windows and doors against the effects of blast.

"I know we aren't supposed to grumble," said Mr. Yasuhara, "but I wish they'd tell us how we're meant to put up these wretched boards. I'll not get anywhere at this rate. There's not a single workman left in town and when I went to the iron-monger just now, there wasn't a nail in the shop. I've had to pull the nails out of my own floorboards and make do."

The complaints poured forth monotonously as he hammered away at his door. From inside the shop a clock struck twelve. Turning to me, Mr. Yasuhara said, "Did you know you had a fishhook in your hat, Masu?" He reached out and removed the hook, which must have been there since I went fishing some days before.

"Well, I shan't keep you from your hammering any longer," I said. "I don't suppose there's all that much time for us to get out of here."

Next I called at the Kobayashi Inn, opposite the station, which I had known for over thirty years. During my student days I had always stayed there while traveling between Tokyo and my parents' home in the country, and since then I had made it my headquarters whenever I visited Fukuyama. In the courtyard behind the inn was an old plum tree and at its roots an Imbe-ware water jar. I remembered this jar standing in the same place ever since my school days. It was a dark clay jar about four feet high and glazed a vermilion in color; on one side, six lines intersected each other in a pattern of naughts-and-crosses.

It was some time now since I had first asked the landlady to sell me the jar, but she had refused on the grounds that she might need it should the water-supply ever be cut off. There was something very attractive about this jar, but it wasn't until the landlady's refusal that I realized how much I had always wanted it. On my next visit to Fukuyama I again made an offer. This time the landlady declined, saying that the jar had been there ever since her father's day. When I mentiond the matter again some months later, she said she could not part with the jar as it was so beautiful in the rain. Since then I had frequently tried to buy it, though never with any real hope of success. But now that we were all to be evacuated, perhaps she would finally part with the jar, which still stood in its place under the plum tree in the courtyard.

"That water jar of yours," I said to the landlady. "What about letting me take it to my village for safekeeping? I know where I can hire a cart for the day, so it will be quite easy for me to move it."

"I never heard that we had to evacuate our water jars," said the landlady. "You don't really suppose they're going to bomb those, do you?" Then with an air of finality she added, "The only thing that's being evacuated from my inn is people."

There was a great crowd at the inn, all waiting for lunch, and the landlady and her assistants were rushing to and fro trying to accommodate them. The rooms upstairs were packed with people and even the annex was crowded. From snatches of conversation, I gathered that the trains bound for Hiroshima on the Tokyo-Hiroshima line were being stopped at the next station and the passengers were being advised to get off at Fukuyama. "Even the railway people don't know what's holding the trains up," I heard the landlord tell one of his customers.

Two men in civilian uniforms were sitting next to the entrance of the dining room complaining about the increasing inefficiency of the State Railways. "They've got no right to push us around like this!" I heard one of them tell his companion. "I went up to the stationmaster himself and said, 'It's your duty to inform us why the Hiroshima trains are being held up.' And all he could say was, 'I don't know, sir, I don't know.' 'No doubt it's your aim in life to reduce your passengers to a state of nervous prostration,' I said to him." "You're quite right," said the other man. "They're a perfect disgrace, these State Railways."

I left the Kobayashi Inn and called at the nearby Hirai Dental Clinic, whose director had been a classmate of mine at middle school. Walking through the crowded waiting room, I found him in his consulting chamber. He was leaning forward with his elbow on a table and his chin resting in his hand.

"Well, well, Masu," he said as he saw me, "so they've finally ordered us to clear out. It's going to be quite a job for us here at the clinic, I can tell you." He threw an unhappy glance around the room. "And what do you suppose will happen to this old town of ours?"

"Oh, I expect the bombers will make a thorough job of it!

What about all your medical equipment?"

"Yes indeed, what about it . . .?" said the director vaguely.

At the other end of the consulting chamber a couple of orderlies were silently attending to some patients. The director appeared to take no interest in them. Just a few days before, his only son, who had volunteered as a junior pilot, had been killed, and this news seemed to have taken all life out of him. I felt that if the air raid siren were to sound this very moment, he would not take shelter but continue to stand there leaning on the table.

After my visit to the clinic, I left Fukuyama on foot, taking the road along the river. As I approached the bottom of the railway bridge, I noticed an emplacement with an anti-aircraft gun surrounded by sandbags. There was not a soldier in sight. The gunbarrel was pointing west towards Hiroshima. I sat down near the deserted emplacement and opened my lunch box, and as I ate, I gazed at the sky around about. I had the feeling that at any moment an enemy plane would appear over the high hills. But no plane came.

Had it not been for those hills, I might have seen the remains of the mushroom cloud over Hiroshima. The inhabitants of Mihara, about seventy miles from Hiroshima, clearly saw the cloud welling up in the blue sky; and the students in the Etajima Military Academy (at about the same distance from the city), who were doing their daily gymnastics, were hurled to the ground at the moment of the bombing. All the academy windows facing Hiroshima were shattered.

In fact I did not hear of the destruction of Hiroshima until about thirty or forty hours after the event. We in our village first learned what had happened indirectly from one of the victims who had fled to the neighboring village. He reported that some strange weapon had been exploded and that from one moment to another the city of Hiroshima had ceased to exist. The victim's name was Kobayashi. He had formerly been the principal of our own village school but had been promoted some years before to the post of director of one of the primary schools in Hiroshima. I knew him from my school days, when he had been in the class ahead of me. He had been a reserved, modest boy. I remember how I had once caught the braid of my school uniform on a nail and he had got it off for me without tearing it.

Rumors of Kobayashi's fate soon reached the village. We heard that on the day Hiroshima was bombed, he was giving lessons at the school. After class he went to his study, but just then there was an air raid warning and he took shelter under his desk. Some minutes later the all-clear siren sounded. Kobayashi stood up. As it was very hot, he took off his coat and went over to the window. He was just removing his shirt when there was a tremendous flash in the sky and he felt the heat going right through his skin. There was a swishing sound and the earth trembled slightly. "The secret weapon!" he thought. He threw on his coat and ran out through the back gate. An empty truck stood directly outside the school, and without thinking, Kobayashi scrambled into the back. An old man hurried out of the house opposite and climbed into the driver's seat. The truck drove off.

Kobayashi had no idea where they were going. He lay silently in the back and before long he fainted. When he came to, he found that they had arrived at some town he did not recognize. He was aware of a peculiar pain throughout his body. Something told him that he was going to die. Whatever happened, he must make his way back to his home village and his family! He managed to get a ride on a truck to Fukuyama and from there an army car took him home. He returned covered with blood. He immediately visited Dr. Tawa, the village doctor, but the latter had no idea how to treat him.

Two days after Hiroshima's destruction, Fukuyama was raided at night. I heard the planes coming over in endless droves.

Later I climbed the hill behind the village and, standing next to a big rock called the Devil's Mortar, watched the glow of the burning town. As Fukuyama was hidden by other hills, I could not see the conflagration directly, but the whole side of one hill was bright with the reflection of the flames. At one place, a huge pillar of fire reared itself over the hill crests. The castle tower must be alight. In a rift between the hills I could see that two large groups of houses outside the town had caught fire. The burning houses made small pinpricks of light across the dark wide plain.

"What can those lights be over there?" I heard someone say. "They look like the flames the fishermen use at night."

Quite a few villagers had come up to watch the burning town. Most of them were silent, and in the dark I could not make out who they were.

"What on earth can those lights be?" the same voice repeated. But no one answered.

After a time, someone shouted from below, "Hey, is anyone up there from the Western Neighborhood Association?" There was no reply. Again the person below shouted, "Hey, up there! All the men from the Western Association are to assemble at once. We're going to Fukuyama to rescue the victims. Come on!"

A few people, who had been squatting by a pine tree, stood up without a word and began scrambling down the hill. As they ran, they looked up nervously now and again at an American plane directly overhead. Its light moved back and forth between our village and Fukuyama; finally it disappeared in the distant black sky. I wondered if the plane had been in the line of fire of the anti-aircraft gun where I had eaten my box lunch; the gun seemed to have been silent all evening.

Finally the pillar of fire disappeared from sight and the pinpricks of light also vanished. I walked slowly down the hill. There had been something uncanny about this raid, which I had stood watching in silence without knowing what was really happening. At the time I had thought that there must be at least two hundred enemy planes, but it turned out that there had been only sixty. Yet about seventy per cent of the town had burned down; an incendiary bomb had entered the castle tower which, after blazing for several hours, had collapsed.

What would the next target be? This was a favorite subject for discussion in our village. By now almost all the cities and big towns on the Inland Sea had been raided. Hiroshima had been destroyed and before that Okayama; Imabari, some distance from the sea, had also been pulverized. Okayama, like Fukuyama, was bathed in incendiary bombs; Imabari and Amagasaki were attacked with high explosives. I remember how during the raid on Amagasaki we could feel the whole earth trembling, even though the town was at a considerable distance from our village. Perhaps because my house was next to a high stone wall, my wife and I were particularly aware of the tremors. We were listening at the time to an eyewitness account of the bombing on the radio and the combination of this direct description with the repeated tremors was quite nerve-racking.

As it happened, there were no more large-scale raids in our area. A week after the attack on Fukuyama, we heard on the radio of our surrender. That day the stomach trouble from which I had been suffering intermittently became acute, and I decided to visit Dr. Tawa in the neighboring village. I found him in a state of great agitation. It appeared that he was having an endless series of calls these days; no sooner had he returned from one round of visits than he would find a new list of patients requiring his immediate attention. All the young men in the area had been enrolled as volunteers and shortly before the attack on Hiroshima had been sent to the city to help in the evacuation. After the atom bomb attack the survivors had made their way back to their villages, most of them horribly burnt or maimed. Even those who were superficially unscathed complained of peculiar pains throughout their bodies.

"It's a funny thing," Dr. Tawa told me. "They can't even tell me exactly where the pain is. All they can say is that it hurts terribly. I can't find anything specifically wrong with them. It must be some new type of illness we don't know anything about and I'm afraid medicine isn't going to do them any good."

As there was yet no medical term for this illness, Dr. Tawa provisionally referred to it as "the volunteers' illness" or "the illness with the peculiar pain." Compared to this illness, of course, my stomach trouble counted for very little in his eyes.

Most of the victims of "the volunteers' illness" who were going to die did so within two weeks. The local paper recommended cauterization with the moxa as a cure. This treatment was used by almost everyone in our region who had been exposed to the atom bomb; some people even used it after contact with the victims, believing the illness to be infectious. I do not know how effective the moxa was, but I heard people swear that it had saved their lives.

Many young men from my own village died that day at Hiroshima. Among them was the son of Mr. Yasuhara, the pharmacist, who had recently started school at Hiroshima. He was killed instantaneously. It was just at the time of the raid that I had stood chatting with his father outside the pharmacy and it occurred to me that at the very moment Mr. Yasuhara removed the fish hook from my hat, his son must have dropped dead. There did not seem to be anything particularly ill-omened in the words, "Did you know you had a fish hook in your hat?" I wondered what Mr. Yasuhara would feel should he ever remember them.

Two days later I went to Fukuyama to see the ruins of the castle tower. I had often read impressive descriptions of burnt towers in historical romances and I was curious to see one in reality. Yet when I reached the site of the castle, nothing remained of the great tower but anonymous heaps of earth and tiles. A few people were digging about in the debris with shovels of pieces of wood, searching for the nails that had supported the ancient gargoyles. Some of the nails had been laid out by the side of the road. They were as big as fire tongs.

Parts of the castle wall were still standing. The huge stones were covered with marks of burning and had turned to a dark clay color. I could feel a warm wind blowing up from the bottom of the wall.

I walked slowly down the hill to the town itself, which was almost completely burned. I visited the remains of the Kobayashi Inn opposite the gutted station. On the door was an evacuation notice giving the landlady's new address. The plum tree in the courtyard had vanished without a trace. The Imbeware water jar still stood there, but was cracked in two right down the middle. It had kept its lovely vermilion color. I sat down on a charred stone and wrote a card to the landlady: "Dear Madam, I hasten to inform you of a lamentable state of affairs. I am writing this card sitting on a charred stone in the burnt ruins of your inn. The water jar which we discussed the other day is broken clean in two. May I now take it to my house for safekeeping? If you prefer, I shall buy it from you for the sum I mentioned. In any case, I am sure you will not want to leave it as it is. I hope you will seriously consider my request and find time to send me a reply as soon as possible. May I take advantage of this note to express my sympathy in your loss? Yours sincerely . . . ."

I intended to post the card on returning to my village, but suddenly changed my mind and threw it away. I was afraid the landlady might think it was written in fun.

The water jar remained where it was for some time. When I went fishing in the beginning of October, I again visited the ruins of the inn and saw the jar still standing there in two pieces. But when I passed through Fukuyama later that month on my way to Iwakuni, I found that it had been pounded into fragments, together with the fallen bricks and debris.

On the train to Iwakuni, I thought about the jar and kept on composing different cards I might send the landlady: "Dear Madam, The image of that bygone water jar haunts me incessantly. How transient, alas, the beauty of this world! Yours sincerely . . . ."

As the train rattled on, I felt more and more exasperated with the landlady. Why couldn't she at least have let me have the jar for safekeeping, even if she didn't want to sell it? My annoyance was aggravated by the fact that I had to stand all the way to Iwakuni, as the train was packed. Passing through Hiroshima, I tried to get a glimpse of the ruins, but could see nothing for the crowds that blocked the train windows. It was not until ten months later that I visited the city. I remember how impressed I was then to find that of all the trees in Hiroshima, the palms alone, though charred and twisted, had withstood the tremendous temperature of a year before and were now putting forth buds.

With the surrender, not only did my stomach trouble continue to get worse but I began to suffer from insomnia. On the evening of the day I had visited the castle tower, a member of our Village Committee brought a notice to my house: "You will proceed to the school playground at Kannabe to receive your share of reserve stores. You will assemble at 5 a.m. tomorrow at the residence of the head of your Neighborhood Association. If you have a truck, wagon, or any other form of conveyance, you will bring it to the place of assembly. At least one member must report from each household."

I went to bed almost at once for fear of being late the following morning. But try as I might, sleep would not come. Indeed, I did not sleep a wink that night, and with bleary eyes and a dull head appeared at the designated spot at five o'clock the next morning. In front of the house a few early arrivals were already kindling a fire and discussing the type of reserve stores which our village was likely to receive.

The Army had stored vast supplies in our district, evidently in the expectation of a prolonged war. They had used almost every conceivable storing place: textile factories which had been forced to close down owing to lack of raw materials, breweries which had suspended operations following the Law Regulating Civilian Enterprises, granaries, soybean warehouses, saké breweries, farms, and even school buildings.

Here they had brought a mass of miscellaneous material whose possible value to the Army was often hard to fathom. In our village school, they had stored a sewing machine in one classroom and huge rolls of paper in another; they had then locked and sealed the doors. In the meadow by the river they had piled rolls of paper in an immense pyramid and covered it with a waterproof tent. Another tent nearby sheltered a wheelbarrow. All private warehouses and storerooms in the area had been requisitioned. In our village the Army had used them for storing jars of wine; they had heaped the jars up to the ceilings, locked the doors and affixed the Army seals. Kannabe had apparently been the center of the Army's storing operations and, according to rumor, the reason that the Americans had destroyed Fukuyama so thoroughly was that they had mistaken it for this nearby town.

Our village had only been able to assemble four wagons. At about six o'clock we set out for Kannabe, taking turns in pulling them. All the villages and hamlets in the three rural districts of our area had been ordered to collect supplies from Kannabe and the narrow country road was packed solidly with wagons, horse carts, wheelbarrows and people. No effort had been made to regulate the traffic. Frequently we would meet groups coming in the opposite direction from Kannabe. Since it was impossible for the wagons and carts to pass each other, we had to lift them above our heads. The shouting and confusion at these moments had to be heard and seen to be believed.

Our group reached the school playground at eight o'clock in the morning, but was forced to wait there until five o'clock in the afternoon before receiving further instructions. After standing for some time in the broiling sun, I went and sat under a tree in the corner of the playground near the school building. In the playground were stacked enormous piles of paper rolls, and sheets of paper the size of carpets. I do not know exactly what was in the schoolhouse, but judging from the loads carried out by people who had gone inside to help themselves, the principal articles were clothing, farm tools, old magazines, and camouflage nets. The clothing consisted of blue shirts for soldiers and overcoats for officers. The blue shirts were in bundles about three to four feet high, loosely tied together with cord.

The shirts seemed to be the most popular booty for the people who went into the schoolhouse to pilfer supplies. As they staggered out with their huge loads, other people standing near the entrance would snatch a couple of shirts from the top of the bundle. The man carrying the shirts couldn't do much about this without dropping his entire bundle. Shouting abuse, he would push his way slowly through the crowd. Then someone else would grab a few more shirts from him and while he was looking to see who it was, still another man would snatch a handful. In the end, the original thief would be left with only two or three shirts.

No one did anything to prevent the pilfering. There were three men outside the school building wearing the armbands of auxiliary Kempei military police, but they seemed quite at a loss as to whether or not they should interfere. They obviously did not know how much power, if any, they retained, now that Japan had surrendered. They have to pretend not to see anything, I thought to myself. At that moment one of the police went up to a man who had stolen a single shirt and snatched it from him. He made the man show him his papers and wrote something in a notebook.

"What do you blasted Kempei think you're doing?" someone shouted from the crowd. "Still trying to throw your weight around?"

A few others took up the cry: "Pretty stuck-up, aren't you?" "Remember, you've had your day now!"

Just then there was a sudden agitation among the crowd and lots of people ran and hid behind the wagons. I looked up. The sky was full of what seemed to be sparkling gray missiles flying about in all directions. For a moment I too felt panic; then I realized that they were just scraps of burning paper being blown about in the wind. It turned out that the employees of the District Office were burning part of the archives and were throwing them out of the window. Conditioned as we all were by the fear of air raids, they had appeared to us like some terrible new weapon.

After we had waited for nine hours in the school playground, our group was ordered to proceed to the square in front of the main saké brewery of the town. Here again we waited. As I was sleepy, I sat down on one of the wagons and dozed off. When I awoke, it was already dark. We had eaten our box-lunches hours before. Hungry and exhausted, we waited in silence outside the saké brewery.

We had become accustomed to this sort of treatment during the war and it occurred to me that it was to become part of our lives in peacetime as well. Midnight had passed when we were moved to still another waiting place, and by this time I was too tired to take in much that was happening. I remember that we all gathered by a wagon beside the road, joining groups from several other villages. One group loaded hundreds of sheets of paper on to horse carts and then set off silently into the night.

After waiting another two hours, we were instructed to load

one of our wagons with two paper rolls and the other with printing paper, blue shirts, uncut material for Army uniforms, and shovels. Then at last we were told to return home. Dawn was breaking as we entered the village before ours and, dizzy with exhaustion, I had fallen out of the ranks. A group from a distant mountain village passed as I stood by the side of the road. I noticed that all their carts were loaded with printing ink. "What on earth do they expect us to do with this stuff?" one of the men said, looking in my direction with a weary smile.

Next day we were summoned to the village hall for the distribution of reserve stores. The tinned food, clothing, and shovels were equitably divided; the printing paper was also shared out—so many sheets per family. The paper rolls, however, presented some difficulty. After lengthy discussion, it was decided to divide one of the rolls, a job that was entrusted to the village carpenter. Instead of unrolling the paper and measuring off a number of equal lengths with a ruler, the man took a cleaver and hacked away at the full roll. The pieces of paper that emerged were mangled and of different sizes, those coming from the center of the roll being, of course, much smaller. The Village Committee then called for a scale and distributed the paper by weight. The disposal of the second roll was left for future decision.

As soon as I knew of the surrender, I decided to return to Tokyo. It was about a week after the raid on Fukuyama that I visited my friend Mr. Masahiko Kiuchi, who had been evacuated from Tokyo at the same time as myself, to discuss plans. He was living with his wife in a small annex next to her parents' house on the outskirts of Fukuyama. Here I spent the night. From the second floor one could look out to the sea in the south and to the mountains in the west. Directly below the window was a pond. In the evening I played chess with my friend but soon became tired and went to bed, falling asleep instantly without my usual insomnia.

I awoke at early dawn, got up and opened the window. It was then that I saw a strange sight in the pond. I hurriedly fetched the bed lamp and, extending the flex to the window, pointed it in the direction of the water. I took one look and turned out the light. I closed the window. What I had seen floating on the surface was a human body. The iris were clustered at one end of the pond and a few yards away was something that looked like a piece of purple tissue paper. The body was floating on its back, one cheek almost touching the purple object.

I could not wait for the others to wake up and ran downstairs shouting for Mr. Kiuchi.

"Don't tell me you're awake already, Masu," I heard his wife's sleepy voice coming from their bedroom.

"I'll be right up," said Mr. Kiuchi.

I returned to my room and waited. A few minutes later he joined me in his pajamas, seeming half asleep. "I'm sorry I had to wake you," I said, "but there's something terrible floating on the pond down there."

Kiuchi walked towards the window and then suddenly stopped. "No, I'd rather not see," he said. "There's no point in my looking . . . . Has someone drowned?"

"Yes. You'll have to notify the police right away. I think it's a woman. I saw it just now when I was opening the window."

"All right. I'll go next door and phone for the police."

He ran downstairs and almost at once his wife came up.

"How awful!" she said. "Who can it be?"

"I don't know. I don't want to look again. It wasn't there yesterday afternoon. It must have come to the surface after dark."

"In that case, whoever it was, drowned a week ago. They say it takes a week for the body to start floating."

A week, I thought—so she must have been drowned the day Fukuyama was raided.

I was washing my face when my friend returned. "They'll be along right away," he said.

"Hey, Masahiko, are you sure it wasn't here yesterday?" We heard the voice of Mrs. Kiuchi's father from down below by the pond. My friend went up to the window but did not look out. "Yes, Father, I'm quite sure," he shouted. "Someone would have seen it . . . . I don't know how you can bear to stand there staring at it," he added.

"Did you know there is an iris in bloom?" the old man's voice came up. "It's amazing! Think of an iris blooming at this time of year! Here, have a look!" But Mr. Kiuchi still would not peer out of the window.

After breakfast a police officer and a detective arrived. They took down a detailed statement from us and then examined the scene of the drowning, neither Kiuchi nor I accompanying them. When they returned to the house, they told us they had found a woman's sandal nearby. Perhaps, they said, the victim had been terrified by the air raid and in a fit of hysteria run headlong from the town. Overcome by emotion, she may have leaped into the pond. Their examination of the body had revealed a burn on the cheek, which obviously lent credence to this theory. The girl was about twenty years old and was wearing an old nightgown tied with a red sash.

After the police had left, Mrs. Kiuchi heated a bath for me in the main house. As soon as I lay in the hot water, I fell asleep and it was afternoon before I awoke. Mr. Kiuchi had come in and was shaking me by the shoulders.

"Well, Masu, you can look at the pond now, if you like. The ambulance came for the body while you were asleep."

"Was it a murder or a suicide?" I asked.

"I gather she was a half-crazy girl. Her parents had sent her to Hiroshima to work in a factory and she was there when the atom bomb exploded. She got back to Fukuyama the day it was bombed. This second raid seems to have been too much for her. She went clean off her rocker!"

Returning to my room, we both looked out of the window. The pond was a rectangle about a hundred yards across, with water flowing in from a stream at one end and pouring out into a small gully. At the mouth of the gully was clustered the main group of irises; a few feet away grew the angular leaves from whose recess emerged the twisted stem with its belated, purple flowers. The petals looked hard and crinkly. No wonder I had mistaken them for tissue paper.

"Do you think that iris was frightened into bloom?" I said.

"It's extraordinary," said Kiuchi. "I've never heard of an iris flowering this late. It must have gone crazy!"

Suddenly it came back to me. It may have been something I had once heard, or perhaps part of a story I had read. This iris it was that now brought the incident to my mind.

A young man—a writer I think he was—had lodgings in a house near Tokyo and from his window he could look out on a pond like this one. In a corner of the pond grew a cluster of iris in full bloom. Not far away stood a miserable hovel in which lived a young cabinetmaker and his younger sister. The girl was unmarried. She went away to work as a maid for some family and returned pregnant.

One morning, when the writer happened to look out of his window, he saw the girl floating face upwards on the pond near where the iris grew. She was wearing a beautiful kimono whose sleeves hovered on the surface of the water like the fins of a goldfish. When the cabinetmaker found his sister, he knelt down by the pond and stretched out his hand to her body. He took one of her arms and gently placed it over her swollen stomach; then he took her other arm and placed it on her stomach in the same way, so that one hand lay ceremoniously over the other and the wide sleeves covered her body. After this, he hurried away.

When I told Mr. Kiuchi this incident, he turned to me and

said, "There's all the difference in the world, you know, between the iris in your story and the flower down there in the pond. They belong to completely different periods. The iris blooming in this pond is crazy and belongs to a crazy age!"

translated by Ivan Morris

NOTE

Dr. Morris's translation of "The Crazy Iris" was published some years ago and is reproduced here with minor changes. (Ed.)

Tamiki Hara

Summer Flower

I went downtown and bought some flowers, thinking I would visit the grave of my wife. In my pocket I had a bundle of incense sticks that I had taken from the Buddhist altar in my home. August 15 would be the first anniversary for the soul of my wife, but it was doubtful whether my native town would survive until then. Although most factories were closed that day due to electric power rationing, there was no one to be seen except myself—walking along the street with flowers, in the early morning. I did not know the name of the flowers, but they looked like a summer variety with the rustic beauty of their tiny yellow petals.

As I sprayed water over the gravestone exposed to the scorching heat of the sun, divided the flowers into two bunches and put them in the vases on either side, the grave appeared rather refreshing, and I gazed at the flowers and the stone for a while. Underneath the grave were buried not only the ashes of my wife but also those of my parents. After burning the incense sticks that I had brought and making a bow, I drank out of the well beside the grave. Then I went home by way of Nigitsu Park. The scent of the incense remained in my pocket throughout that day and the next. It was on the third day after my visit to the grave that the bomb was dropped.

My life was saved because I was in the bathroom. On the

morning of August 6, I had gotten up around eight o'clock. The air-raid alarm had sounded twice the night before and nothing had happened, so that before dawn I had taken off my clothes and slept in my night robe, which I had not put on for a long time. Such being the case, I had on only my shorts when I got up. My younger sister, when she saw me, complained of my rising late, but I went into the bathroom without replying.

I do not remember how many seconds passed after that. All of a sudden, a powerful blow struck me and darkness fell before my eyes. Involuntarily I shouted and held my hands over my head. Aside from the sound of something like the crashing of a storm, I could not tell what it was in the complete darkness. I groped for the door, opened it, and found the veranda. Until then, I had been hearing my own voice exclaiming, "Wah!" amid the rushing sounds, agonized at not being able to see. But after I came out to the veranda, the scene of destruction gradually loomed in the dusk before my eyes and I became clearly conscious.

It looked like an episode from a loathsome dream. At first, when the blow struck my head, and I lost my sight, I knew that I had not been killed. Then I became angry, thinking that things had become very troublesome. And my own shouts sounded almost like the voice of somebody else. But when I could see, vaguely as it was, the things around me, I felt as if I were standing stage center in a tragic play. Certainly I had beheld such a scene in a movie. Beyond the clouds of dust, patches of blue sky began to come into view. Light came in through holes in the walls and from other unexpected directions. As I walked gingerly on the boards where the tatami flooring had been blown off, my sister came rushing toward me. "You weren't hurt? You weren't hurt? Are you all right? Your eyes are bleeding. Go wash right away." She told me that there was still water running in the kitchen scullery.

Finding myself completely naked, I turned to my sister and

asked her, "Can you at least get me something to put on?" She was able to pull out a pair of shorts from the closet that had been saved from destruction. Someone rushed in with a bewildered gesture. His face was smeared in blood. He wore only a shirt. This man was an employee of a nearby factory. Seeing me, he said, "It's lucky you were saved." Then he bustled away, muttering, "Telephone . . . . I have to make a telephone call."

There were crevices everywhere, and the doors, screens, and tatami mats were scattered about. The pillars and doorsills were clearly exposed, and the whole building was filled with a strange silence. Later I was told that most houses were completely destroyed in that area, but my second floor did not give way; even the floor boards remained firm. My father, a painstaking builder, had built our house about forty years before, and it had been solidly constructed.

Tramping about over the littered mats and screens, I looked among scattered articles for something to wear. The book which I had left half read the night before was there on the floor with its pages turned up. The picture frame which had fallen from the beam overhead stood tinged with death in front of the *tokonoma*. I found my canteen quite unexpectedly, and then my hat. Still unable to find my pants, I started looking for something else to cover myself.

K of the factory office appeared on the veranda of the drawing room. Seeing me, he cried in a sad voice, "I'm hurt! Help me!" and dropped down in a heap where he stood. Blood was oozing from his forehead, and his eyes were glistening with tears.

"Where is it?" I asked, and he distorted his pale wrinkled face, saying, "My knees," as he held them with his hand. I gave him a strip of cloth, and I drew over my own legs two pairs of socks, one over the other.

"It's started to smoke. Let's get out of here. Help me get

away." K, who was considerably older than I but usually much more vigorous, seemed to be highly disturbed.

Looking out from the veranda, I could see nothing recognizable except the clusters of flattened houses and a ferroconcrete building a little farther away. Beside the toppled-over mud wall there was a tall maple tree whose trunk was torn off halfway up; the twigs had been thrown into the wash basin. Suddenly K stopped by the air-raid shelter, and said, "Why don't we stay here? There's a water tank, besides . . . ." When I said, "No, let's go to the river," he asked me wonderingly, "The river? Which direction is the river?"

I took a night robe out of the closet, handed it to him, and tore the shelter curtain. I picked up a cushion, too. When I turned the mat on the veranda, I found my emergency bag. I felt relieved and put the bag on my shoulder. Small red flames rose from the warehouse of the chemical factory next door. We went out over the completely twisted maple.

That tall tree had stood in the corner of the garden for a long time, and had been an object of dreamy imagination in my childhood. Recently I had come back and started living at my own home after a long time, and now I thought it odd that even this tree did not evoke the same old sweet memory. What was strange was that my home town itself had lost its soft natural atmosphere, and I felt it to be something like a composition of cruel, inorganic matter. Every time I went into the drawing room facing the garden, the title, *The Fall of the House of Usher*, spontaneously sprang to my mind.

K and I climbed over the crumbling houses, clearing obstacles from our path, and walked slowly at first. We came to level ground, and knew that we were on the road, where we walked faster down the middle. Suddenly there called a voice from behind a crushed building, crying, "Please!" Turning back, I found that the voice belonged to a woman with a blood-stained face walking toward us. "Help me!" she cried, following us desperately. We had walked on for some time when we passed an old woman who stood in the middle of the path with her legs wide apart. She was crying like a child, "The house is catching fire! The house is catching fire!" Smoke rose here and there from the crumbling houses, and suddenly we came upon a spot where breaths of flame belched furiously.

We passed it running. The road became level again, and we found ourselves at the foot of Sakae Bridge. Here the refugees gathered one after another. Someone who had stationed himself on the bridge cried out: "Those who are strong enough, put out the fire!" I walked toward the grove of Asano Park, and there became separated from K.

The bamboo grove had been mowed down, and a path made through the grove under the tramping feet of refugees. Most of the trees overhead had been torn apart in midair, and this famous old garden on the river was now disfigured with pockmarks and gashes. Beside a hedge was a middle-aged woman, her ample body slumped over limply. Even as I looked, something infectious seemed to emanate from her lifeless face. It was the first such face I had seen. But I was to see many, many more that were more grotesque.

In the grove facing the riverbank I came across a group of students. These girls had escaped from a factory, and all had been injured slightly, but now, trembling from the freshness of the thing that had happened before their very eyes, they chattered excitedly. At that moment my eldest brother appeared. He wore only a shirt, but looked unhurt. He had a beer bottle in one hand. The houses on the other bank of the river had collapsed and were on fire, but the electric poles still stood. Sitting on the narrow road by the riverbank, I felt I was all right now. What had been threatening me, what had been destined to happen, had taken place at last. I could consider myself as one who survived. I have to keep a record of this, I said to myself. But I scarcely knew the truth about the air raid then.

The fire on the opposite bank of the river raged more furiously. The scorching heat reached this side of the river, so that we had to dip the cushion in the rising water and put it over our heads. Then someone shouted, "Air raid! People with white clothing should hide under the trees!" All the people crowded into the heart of the grove.

The sun sent forth its bright rays, and the other side of the grove seemed to be on fire. A hot wind blew overhead, and black smoke was fanned up toward the middle of the river. Then the sky suddenly grew dark, and large drops came down in torrents. The rain reduced the heat momentarily, but soon the sky cleared up again. The fire on the other bank was still burning. Over on this side, my eldest brother, my younger sister, and a couple of people from our neighborhood whose faces I recognized had appeared. We got together and talked about what had happened that morning.

My brother had been seated at a table in his office when a flash of light raced through the garden. The next instant, he was blown some distance from his seat and for a while found himself squirming around under the wreckage of the house. At last he discovered an opening and succeeded in crawling out. From the direction of the factory he could hear the student workers screaming for help, and he went off to do what he could to rescue them.

My sister had seen the flash of light from the entrance hall and had rushed as fast as she could to hide under the stairs. As a result, she had suffered little injury.

Everyone had at first thought that just his own house had been hit by a bomb. But then when they went outside and saw that it was the same everywhere, they were dumfounded. They were also greatly puzzled by the fact that, although the houses and other buildings had all been damaged or destroyed, there didn't seem to be any holes where the bombs had fallen. The air raid warning had been lifted, and shortly after that there had been a big flash of light and a soft hissing sound like magnesium burning. The next they knew everything was turned upside down. It was all like some kind of magical trick, my sister said, trembling with terror.

The fire on the opposite bank had no sooner begun to die down when someone said that the trees in the garden on this side of the river had caught fire. We could see wisps of smoke rising in the sky behind the grove. The water in the river remained at high tide and did not recede.

I walked along a stone embankment down to the water's edge and discovered a large wooden box floating along at my feet, and around it bobbed onions that had spilled out. Pulling the box to me, I took out the onions and handed them to people on the bank. The box had been thrown out of a freight train which had been overturned on the bridge upstream. While I was picking up the onions, there came a voice crying, "Help!" Clinging to a piece of wood, a young girl drifted in the middle of the river, floating at one time and sinking at another. I took a large timber and swam toward her pushing it. Although I had not swum for a long time, I managed to help her more easily than I had expected.

The fire on the opposite bank, which had slackened for a while, had started raging again. This time, murky smoke mingled with the red flames, and as the roiling mass expanded, the heat of the flames seemed to grow more intense with each second. When the fire finally burned itself out, there remained only an empty carcass. It was then that I sensed a wall of air undulating toward us over the water. Tornado! Even as the thought struck me, a blast of wind passed over our heads. The grass and trees around me trembled, and whole trees were plucked out and snatched high into the air. I don't remember exactly what color the air around us was at that time. I think it must have been wrapped in a kind of weird greenish glow, the kind you see in pictures of Hell.

When the tornado had passed, the sky showed that evening was near. My second elder brother appeared quite unexpectedly. His shirt was torn in back, and there was a brushing trace the color of thin India ink on his face which later became a suppurating burn. Coming home on business, he had sighted a small airplane in the sky and then three strange flashes. After being thrown on the ground, he had run to rescue his wife and the maid-servant, who were struggling under the collapsed house. He entrusted his two children to the maid and let them escape before him, and then spent much time in saving the old man who lived next door.

His wife had been worrying about the children who had gone off with the maid when she heard the maid shouting to her from the opposite bank. The maid said her arms hurt so much she couldn't carry the children any longer and she wanted someone to come and help her right away.

The grove of Asano Park was little by little catching fire. If night came on and the fire reached the part of the grove where we were, we would be in trouble, so we thought we had better cross over to the other bank while it was still light. But where we were there was no boat to ferry us across. My eldest brother and his group decided to go around by way of the bridge, but my second elder brother and I walked upstream, still hoping to find a ferryboat. The sinking sun made everything around us look pale, and both on and beneath the bank there were pale people who cast their sinister shadows on the water. Their faces were so puffy and swollen you could hardly tell whether they were men or women, with eyes that were mere slits and horribly blistered lips. They lay on their sides, their painful limbs exposed, barely breathing. When we passed before them, these strange people spoke to us in faint, gentle voices, "Give us some water."

Someone called me in a sharp, pitiful voice. Below I saw a

naked young boy whose lifeless body was completely sunk in the water, and two women squatting on the stone steps less than four feet from the corpse. Their faces were swollen twice their natural size, distorted in an ugly way, and only their scorched rumpled hair showed that they were women. Looking at them, I shuddered rather than felt pity. But the women had noticed me. "That mattress over by those trees is ours. Would you be good enough to bring it over here?" they pleaded.

Looking over at the trees, I saw that there was in fact a mattress there. But a man who looked like he was mortally wounded was lying on it, so there was nothing I could do.

My brother and I found a little raft, untied the rope, and rowed toward the opposite bank of the river. Daylight had already turned dusky when the raft reached the sand beach on the other side, and the area was scattered with wounded townsmen. A soldier who was squatting by the river said to me, "Let me drink some hot water." I had him lean against my shoulder and we walked together. As he staggered on the sand, the soldier muttered, "It's much better to be killed." I made him wait beside the path.

Nearing a water supply station I beheld the large burned head of a human being slowly drinking hot water out of a cup; the enormous face seemed to be made up of black soybeans; and the hair above the ears was burned off in a straight line where the man's cap had not protected it. I filled a cup and took it to the soldier. As I did so, I saw another soldier, badly wounded, down on his knees in the river, bending over and intently lapping up the river water.

People were starting to cook their supper, burning pieces of wood on the sandy beach. For some time now, I had been aware of a girl with a terribly swollen face lying close by my side and begging for water. After a while, it dawned on me that it was the maid from my second elder brother's house, the one who had gone off with the children and had earlier been calling for help. She had just been going out the kitchen door with the baby strapped on her back when the blinding flash had come and her face and hands and breast had been burned. My brother had sent her off ahead of him with the baby and the older girl, but when she got to the bridge, she somehow lost the older girl. Still carrying the baby, she had made her way down here to the riverbed. When the flash came, she had held up her hand to shield her face, and now the hand hurt her so much she felt like tearing it off, she said.

As the tide began to rise, we all moved up the bank. Night had fallen, and a breeze sprang up. It was too cool for us to sleep, and we kept hearing voices here and there crying desperately for water. Nigitsu Park was nearby but it was now wrapped in darkness, and we could see only faintly the broken trees. My brothers lay in a hollow in the ground and I placed myself in another shallow place. Close to me lay three or four wounded schoolgirls. "The grove over there has started burning," someone said. "Don't you think we'd better move away from here?" Getting out of the hollow, I saw flames glaring over the top of the trees ahead of us, but there was no sign of the fire spreading up to our spot.

"Does it look as though the fire is going to come over this way?" a wounded girl asked in a frightened voice. When I assured her it was all right, she said, "I wonder what time it is now. Do you think it's twelve o'clock yet?"

There must still have been an undamaged siren somewhere, for we heard its warning faint in the distance.

"I wish morning would come!" one of the schoolgirls complained.

A chorus of soft voices could be heard calling, "Mother! Father!" "Does it look as though the fire is coming over this way?" the wounded girl asked again.

From the direction of the riverbed came death cries, in a young voice still strong. "Water! Water! Please . . . .! Mother . . . . Sister . . . . Mitchan . . . . !" The agonized words, interspersed with moans and weak gasps of pain, seemed to wrench his whole body. One time when I was little I walked along the embankment here and came to the riverbed to catch fish. The memory of that hot summer day remains strangely vivid in my mind. There was a big billboard stuck up in the sand advertising Lion toothpaste, and every now and then from the direction of the railway bridge came the rumble of a passing train. It was a peaceful scene that now seemed like a dream.

By the time morning came, the voices from the night before had ceased, though the piercing death cries that had wrung my heart still rang in my ears. As the scene gradually brightened, a morning breeze began to blow. My eldest brother and my sister went off in the direction where our house had stood, saying they would make their way from there to the East Parade Ground, having heard that a dispensary had been set up there. My second elder brother and his family started off for the East Parade Ground too. I was about to set out for the parade ground myself, when a soldier nearby asked if I would take him with me. He was a big man, and he must have been badly wounded, because he hung on my shoulder and dragged his feet gingerly along the ground as though they were broken things. We had to pick our way among formidable obstacles, shattered glass here, corpses there, objects that were still hot and smoldering. By the time we got to Tokiwa Bridge, the soldier said he was too exhausted to go another step and asked me to leave him there. I did as he told me and went off alone in the direction of Nigitsu Park.

Here and there were houses that had collapsed but had escaped the fire, and everywhere were the scars of that flash of light that had raked over the scene. In an empty lot a crowd of people had gathered. A trickle of water was leaking from the water main. It was there that I chanced to learn that my niece—my second elder brother's child who had gotten separated from the maid yesterday—was safe at the refugee area in the Tōshōgū Shrine.

I hurried off to the garden of the shrine, and came on my little niece just as she and her mother had found each other. The day before, after becoming separated from the maid at the bridge, she had gone off with some other people and made her way here. Now, when she caught sight of her mother, the strain was suddenly too much for her and she burst out wailing. Her head was black and painful looking from burns.

A dispensary had been established near the entrance to the Tōshōgū Shrine. With each case a policeman formally asked the patient his permanent address and age; and the patient, even after receiving a slip of paper identifying him, still had to wait about an hour in a long row, under the scorching sun. Patients who were able to join that row were more fortunate than the rest. Now someone cried furiously, "Soldier! Soldier! Help me! Soldier!" A horribly burned young girl rolled in anguish on the roadside. And near her was a man in the uniform of an air defense guard, who complained in feeble voice, "Please help me, ah, Nurse, Doctor!" as he laid his head, swollen and bloated with burns, on a stone, and opened his blackened mouth. No one gave heed to him. Policemen, doctors, and nurses came from other towns to help, but they were rather few in number.

The maid from my elder brother's family had come to the dispensary with my brother and I helped her to join the row of persons awaiting treatment. Her face and hands were getting more and more swollen and she seemed to want to squat on the ground. When her turn finally came and she had finished being treated, we had to look around for some place to rest. Everywhere we looked in the grounds of the shrine there were wounded people, but there was nothing like a tent or a thicket of trees where we could take shelter. Finally we propped some thin pieces of lumber up against the stone fence surrounding the shrine to make a kind of roof and crawled in under them. For the next twenty-four hours, this cramped space was home for the six of us, my second elder brother and his wife, their two girls, the maid and myself.

Right next to us someone had set up a similar kind of shelter where a man moved around briskly on a piece of matting. Presently he struck up a conversation with us. He had no shirt or undershirt, and all that was left of his trousers was a piece around his waist and part of one leg. His arms, his legs and his face were burned. He said he had been on the seventh floor of the Chūgoku Building when the explosion came, and we could see he had been injured in the blast. He must have had great presence of mind, however, as he had asked people to help him and had somehow managed to flee all the way here.

About that time, a young man with a military cadet's belt, his body smeared all over with blood, pushed his way into the man's shelter. The man was incensed. "Here, here! Get out of here! As sore as I am, I'm not going to have you bumping into me! There're any number of other places you can go—why do you want to squeeze in here! Come on now, get out!" he spluttered in a voice like a bark. The blood-smeared youth got to his feet with a dazed look.

A few yards away from us, two schoolgirls lay groaning for water under a cherry tree, faces burned black, their thin shoulders exposed to the scorching sun. They were students of the girls' commercial school who had met the disaster while potato digging in the vicinity. A woman in work trousers whose face had been smoke-dried joined them. Placing her handbag on the ground, she stretched out her legs listlessly, oblivious to the dying girls. The day was drawing to a close. When I thought of spending another night in a place like this, I became strangely uneasy.

The second night dragged by. Before dawn some unknown voice took up a Buddhist invocation, a sound suggesting that people were dying all the time. The two commercial students died when the morning sun was high. A policeman, when he had finished examining the girls' bodies lying face down in the ditch, approached the dead woman in work trousers nearby. He opened her handbag and found a savings passbook and public loan bonds in it. She still wore the traveling suit in which she had been struck.

About noon, the air-raid warning sounded again and the roar of planes was heard. Although I had become used to the ugliness and misery around me, my fatigue and hunger became more and more intense. My second elder brother's two sons were off at school in the city when the disaster occurred and we still did not know what had happened to them. People died one after another, and their bodies were left as they were. Men walked restlessly, without hope of assistance.

The desperate clarion call of the bugle came from the parade ground. Meanwhile, my brother's little girls sobbed miserably from their burns and the maid kept constantly begging for water. And then, just as I thought we were coming to the end of our endurance, my eldest brother appeared. He had stopped the previous day at Hatsukaichi, to which his sister-in-law had evacuated, and had hired a wagon. He was here with the wagon now, ready to take us away.

My second elder brother, his family, my sister, who had meanwhile joined us, and I all got in the wagon and we left the Tōshōgū Shrine and went toward Nigitsu. As we were going from Shirashima past the entrance of Asano Garden, my second elder brother caught sight of a body in the vacant lot toward the West Parade Ground. It was clothed in yellow pants that were familiar to him. It was Fumihiko, his son. Fluid flowed from a swelling on the boy's breast the size of a fist. His white teeth were dimly visible in his blackened face, and the fingers of both hands were bent inward with the nails boring into the skin. Beside him sprawled the body of a schoolboy and that of a young woman. They lay slightly apart. Both had become rigid in their last positions. My second elder brother stripped off Fumihiko's nails and his belt for a keepsake. Placing a name card on him, we left the spot. It was an encounter too sad for tears.

The wagon then passed Kokutaiji Temple and Sumiyoshi Bridge, and came to Koi, giving me an almost full view of the burned sites of the busiest quarters. Amid the vast, silvery expanse of nothingness that lay under the glaring sun, there were the roads, the river, the bridges, and the stark naked, swollen bodies. The limbs of these corpses, which seemed to have become rigid after struggling in their last agony, had a kind of haunting rhythm. In the scattered electric wires and countless wrecks there was embodied a spasmodic design in nothingness. The burnt and toppled streetcar and the horse with its huge belly on the ground gave me the impression of a world described by a Dali surrealist painting. The tall camphor tree in the precincts of Kokutaiji Temple had been felled completely, and the gravestones too were scattered. The Asano Library, with only its outer block left, had been turned into a morgue. The roads were still smoky here and there and were permeated with a cadaverous smell. Somehow it seems that impressions of the scene are more aptly put in *katakana*:*

The strange rhythm of the human bodies,
    inflamed and red,
That mingle with the glaring wrecks
    and the cinders of grayish white
In the vast panorama—
Is this all that has happened, or is it
    what could have happened?
Oh, the world stripped of all in an
    instant.
How the swollen belly of the horse

glares beside the toppled streetcar.

And the stench of the smoldering wires!

The wagon proceeded along the endless road through the debris. Even on the outskirts of the city, the houses all had collapsed, and it was only after we had passed Kusatsu that we were at last liberated from the shadow of disaster and were greeted by the sight of living green. The appearance of the dragonflies that flitted so swiftly above the emerald rice paddies was touchingly refreshing to my eyes. From here stretched a long, monotonous road to Yawata Village. Night had fallen by the time we reached there, and all was dismally quiet.

The next day, our miserable life—of the aftermath—truly began. The wounded did not recover satisfactorily, and even those who at first had been strong gradually grew weak from lack of food. Our maid's arm suppurated badly, and flies gathered around the burned part, which finally became infested with maggots. No matter how often we sterilized the area, the maggots never ceased to infest the wound. She died a little more than a month later.

Four or five days after we had moved to the village, my nephew, who had been last seen on his way to school, suddenly reappeared. On the morning that he had gone to his school—his building later was to be evacuated—he had seen the flash from inside his classroom. In an instant he hid himself under the desk, and was buried under the falling ceiling, but crawled out through a crevice. There were only four or five boys who had escaped—the rest were killed by the first blow. The survivors ran toward Hiji Hill, and he vomited white fluid on the way. Then he went to the home of one of his friends with whom he had escaped, and there he was sheltered. About a week after his return, my nephew's hair began to fall out, and his nose bled. His doctor declared that his condition was already critical, but my nephew gradually gained his strength again.

My friend N suffered a different experience. He was on his way to visit an evacuated factory, and his train had just entered a tunnel. As the train came out, he saw three parachutes floating down through the air over Hiroshima several miles behind. Arriving at the next station, he was surprised to find that the window glasses were broken. By the time he reached his destination, detailed information already had been circulated. He took the first train back to Hiroshima. Every train that passed was filled with people grotesquely wounded. When he arrived at the town, he could not wait until the fire was quenched, and so he proceeded along the still hot asphalt road.

He went first to the girls' high school where his wife was teaching. On the site of the classrooms lay the bones of the pupils, and on the site of the principal's office lay bones that seemed to have belonged to the principal. Nothing could he identify as the remains of his wife. He hurried back to his own home. Being near Ujina, the house had crumbled without burning. Yet he could not find his wife there either. Then he examined all the bodies lying on the road that led from his home to the girls' school. Most of the bodies were lying on their faces, so that he had to turn them over with his hands in order to examine them. Every woman had been changed miserably, but his wife's body was not there. Finally he wandered around without direction. He saw some ten bodies heaped in a pile in a cistern.

Then there were three bodies that had become rigid as they held a ladder set against the riverbank, and others stood waiting in a row for the bus, the nails of each fastening against the shoulders of the one ahead. The terrible scene of the West Parade Ground was beyond description. There were piles of soldier corpses all around—but the body of his wife was not to be found anywhere.

My friend N visited all the barracks, and looked into the faces of the severely wounded people. Every face was miserable beyond words, but none of the faces was his wife's. After looking for three days and nights at so many charred bodies, dead and living, N at last went back to the burned site of his wife's school.

translated by George Saitō

* *Katakana* characters are much simpler and starker in appearance than the other forms used in writing Japanese.

NOTE

Mr. Saitō's translation of "Summer Flower" was done some years ago from a slightly shortened version of the text. With his permission the editor has added translations of the parts earlier omitted so as to make the translation complete. (Ed.)

Tamiki Hara

The Land of Heart's Desire

(1951) *Musashino City*

CLOSE to dawn I lie in bed, listening to the singing of the birds. They're up there, on the roof of the apartment, singing to me. The rise and fall of their voices, muffled, gentle yet piercing, quivers with sweet anticipation. Are they, perhaps, aware of this most subtle of all moments and innocently signalling its advent to each other? Abed, I chuckle to myself: at this rate, I shall soon be understanding the language of the birds. Yes, just a little more, only a little, and I might well understand it. Suppose, in the next life, I were reborn as a bird and went to visit the land of the birds—what kind of reception would they give me? Would I, even then, stand chewing my fingers in the corner, like some retiring child taken to kindergarten for the first time? Or would I slowly proceed to survey my surroundings with the melancholy, jaundiced eye of a poet? But no—how could I possibly do such things when I was already transformed into a bird? Suddenly, I am on a path through a wood beside a lake, encountering those who were once close to me and are now birds. *Well! You too! . . . What? You here too . . . ?*

I lie in bed as though under a spell, sunk in contemplation of things that could never be. Those once dear to me will never, I feel sure, perish from my life. I must go on living in innocence like the birds, till the moment when death carries me off . . . .

Is my whole being even now, then, still shattered into fragments, swept away into the infinite distance? It is a year already since I moved to these lodgings; and, where I am concerned, human solitude has, I feel sure, all but plumbed the depths. The world no longer affords a single grubby straw for me to clutch at; that is why the stars in the night sky that hang so unconcernedly canopied over my head, and the forms of the trees standing so aloof from me here below, have gradually drawn closer to where I am, as though eventually to take my place. However deep in the slough I may lie at the moment, however chilled to the core, those stars and trees—I tell myself—stand there undaunted, brimming over with something that knows no end . . . . I actually discovered a star of my own. One night, on the dark way from Kichijoji station to my lodgings, something made me glance up at the starry sky above, and there it was—a single star amidst all its innumerable fellows that held my eye and nodded in my direction. What could it mean, I wondered? Yet more important than any meaning was the wave of emotion that brought hot tears to my eyes.

The solitude seems to have become an integral part of the very air. Now that there is no one, they come floating up within me: the little things, such little things . . . . You, my wife, with tears on your eyelashes because something had got in your eye; my mother with a needle, getting a splinter out of my finger . . . . Early one morning I was having a dream about a tooth. And in the dream you came back to me from the dead.

"Where does it hurt?" you asked, and without any fuss ran your finger over the place. The feel of your finger awoke me, and the pain had gone.

I am drifting off to sleep when a sudden shock like lightning strikes my head, which unfolds in an explosion. A sharp spasm seizes my body, then all is still, as though nothing had happened. Opening wide my eyes, I check over my senses: nothing seems to be wrong. What was it then that, independently of my conscious will, had made me explode just now? Where did it come from? *Where?* I don't really know . . . . Could it be all the countless things I have failed to do in my life, bottled up inside me till they exploded? Or could it be the memory of that moment on the morning of the atomic bomb, coming back to assault me after all these years? I cannot really say. So far as I know, the horror of Hiroshima did not affect me mentally. Could it be, though, that the shock of that time has been constantly eyeing me and my fellow victims from a distance, awaiting its chance to drive us mad?

Sleepless in bed, I summon up a vision of the earth. The night cold creeps shuddering into my bed . . . . Why should I be so utterly chilled as this, my body, my existence, my innermost self? I decide to appeal to the earth that gave me being. And dimly, a vision of the earth rises up within me. O wretched globe! O warmthless earth!—Yet this, it seems, is the earth millions of years hence, an earth of which I have as yet no knowledge. And before my eyes there arises, a dim mass, another earth. At the very heart of its sphere, a mass of crimson fire simmers and whirls. What could exist inside a furnace such as that? Substances yet undiscovered, mysteries yet unconceived—such things might well be mingled there. And what will happen to our world when these things spew out, all at once, onto the earth's surface?

All men, I feel sure, have their own vision of the treasures stored beneath the earth, as they face their unknowable future, with its destruction, its salvation . . . . I myself have long cherished a vision of an age when harmony would come to the earth, when deep in men's hearts would sound the quiet murmur of a spring, and there would be nothing to snuff out individual existences any more . . . .

This level crossing is one I often use, and I am frequently

kept waiting when the barrier comes down. Sometimes the train appears from the direction of Nishi-Ogikubo, sometimes it comes from the Kichijoji side. As it draws near, the tracks where I stand develop a perceptible vertical vibration. But then, with a roar, the train goes by at full speed; and the speed leaves me feeling somehow cleansed. Possibly I envy the kind of people who can charge through life at full throttle. But it is others who rise up now before me, men whose eyes are fixed on the tracks with a more despondent gaze. For me, this area along the tracks is haunted constantly by the shadows of those who have come to grief in the world of men—who, writhe and struggle though they may, have been thrust down into the depths of despair. But what of myself as I stand at the crossing, dwelling on such things—has not my own shade too, without my realizing it, come to haunt the same tracks?

One day before sunset I was slowly walking along a main road when suddenly the blue sky took on a strange overall clarity, and for a while a part of it gave off a blue light like mother-of-pearl. I wondered if my eyes had deliberately singled it out. But then my eyes realized that the blue light was pouring down on a neat row of deciduous trees. The trees stood tall and slender; something seemed to be going on in its quiet way. My gaze had just alighted on the uppermost branches of one well-shaped tree when a large, brown withered leaf detached itself from a branch. Leaving the branch, the dead leaf glided straight down along the trunk, to lay itself on other dead leaves piled on the ground at the base. It was a subtly suggestive speed, incomparable to almost anything else. In travelling the distance from the high branch to the ground, the leaf had, I felt sure, taken due note of everything down here on earth . . . . How long was it since I too began to think of taking my own leave of earthly sights? One day, I set out to visit Kanda, where I had lived a year previously. There, spread before my eyes, I found the familiar bustle of the bookstore district. I felt sure, dodging my way through it, that I was somehow looking for my own shadow. On one concrete fence a bare tree and its shadow, pallidly mingled, caught my gaze. Can it really have been that such a pale, hushed happening as this startled my eyes so?

If I'd stayed unmoving in my room I would have frozen stiff, so I went out. The previous night's snow still remained; everything was transformed. As I walked over the snow, my spirits gradually regained their resilience and I began to warm up inside. The cold air cut pleasantly into my lungs. (Yes: the day snow first fell on the ruins of Hiroshima I filled my lungs with just this kind of air, and thrilled with emotion.) It occurred to me that I had not yet written a hymn to snow. How good it would be to tramp vacant-minded, on and on indefinitely, through the snows of the Swiss uplands! Sweet fantasies of death by freezing gripped me. I went into a coffee shop and sat vacantly smoking a cigarette. Bach drifted from a corner of the shop, a gaily decorated iced cake blinked in a glass case. Even if I were to vanish from the world, young men of a similiar temperament to myself would still be sitting in inconspicuous corners of society in just such a way, at just such an hour. I leave the coffee shop and set off along the snowy street again. Few people are about. A lame young man comes trudging from the opposite direction. I feel I know intuitively why he chose to be out walking on a snowy day like this. Never say die, I call to him silently as we pass each other.

Notwithstanding the sight of all our miseries, which press upon us and take us by the throat, we have an instinct which we cannot repress and which lifts us up. (Pascal)

It happened one summer afternoon when I was a child of about six. I was playing by myself on the stone steps of the family's storehouse. To the left of the steps, glittering sunlight tangled with the dense foliage of a cherry tree. It filtered, too, onto the leaves of a *yamabuki* that grew close to the steps. But a pleasantly cool breeze flowed over the top of the steps where I stood bending down. In a kind of ecstasy, I was poking around in the sand on the top of the granite. Suddenly, I noticed a single ant crawling busily toward my hand. Without a thought, I placed a finger firmly on it. The ant, I found, moved no more. After a while, another ant came along. Again, I ground it beneath my finger. One by one the ants came along, and one by one I squashed them. The core of my head grew increasingly heated; time passed in an ecstasy of concentration. Of what I was doing I had no idea at the time. But as the sun set and dusk rose about me, I was plunged without warning into a strange hallucination. I was inside a house. And yet, I did not know where I was. A river of crimson flames swirled and flowed away, then suddenly weird creatures such as I had never seen before were there, gazing at me in the gloom and muttering resentfully in low voices. (Could it be that this dim vision of hell was a foretaste of that second hell I was to be obliged to witness later, at Hiroshima?)

I would have liked to portray a child of unparalleled puniness and oversensitivity; I have feeling that it is the finely-drawn nerves, the nerves liable to snap at the slightest puff of breeze, whose private universe is the worthiest of all.

I wonder if there is a single thing that would raise a genuine smile in my heart? Perhaps, after all, the only thing that would give me relief would be a trifling lyric to the girl. In midsummer the year before last, when I first met her—the girl U—I felt an eerie shudder of the heart, a foreboding that my farewell to things earthly was growing close, that my last years would suddenly come slithering down on top of my head. I could always recall her, that beautiful young girl, with nostalgia and a perfectly pure frame of mind. Whenever I took leave of her, it was like a beautiful rainbow amidst the rain; and I would mentally clasp my fingers together and offer up a private prayer for her happiness.

Once more, a busy sense of things warm and things cold intermingling dazes me with intimations of approaching spring. This enticement of the angels—vital, airy, tender, artful—leaves me vulnerable, threatened by defeat. The flowers burst into bloom, the birds into song, the portents of the dazzling rite are pregnant in the slimmest shaft of sunlight. But something uneasy, something restless begins to flicker in my mind. I see before my eyes the now defunct Flower Festival in the streets of my home town. A picture rises up within me of my dead mother and sisters in their colorful holiday kimono. By now they have a pathetically cute air, almost as though they were young girls. Spring, glorified in verse and painting and music, whispers to me till my head swims. But I remain chill, and slightly sad.

At that period, I am sure, dear, you were trembling on your sickbed with presentiments of the "spring" to come. Now that death was drawing near, everything, no doubt, was crystal clear to you, the bright spaces of heaven close at hand. What dreams, I wonder, were you dreaming then, on your sickbed?

I myself am busily dreaming now—of a lark that rises from the midday wheatfield and soars up into the scorching blue sky . . . . (Could it be your dead self, or is it an image of my own self?) Up and up the lark goes, in a straight line, up and up at full speed, indefinitely. Then, a point reached, it is neither ascending nor descending; life flares up in a bright combustion —the limits of the living transcended, the lark has become a shooting star. (No, it is not me; yet I see in it unmistakably the shape of my heart's desire—if only life had gone in a splendid blaze of beautiful moments lived to the full . . . .)

A Letter to Kiichi Sasaki

I recall with happiness your many kindnesses over the years. My one wish now is to take leave of everything without fuss. Each of my works since the time I lost my wife has been in its own way, I feel, a will.

Seen from the deck of a ship leaving the shore, the land dwindles progressively toward a single point. In the same way my work will become in my eyes a dot, then finally disappear altogether.

I remember the scene last year when Shusaku Endo set off on a voyage to France.

He was looking down at us from the deck of the "Marseille." I and Shigeo Suzuki were exchanging banter on the quayside as we gazed up at the deck with its pre-departure bustle. And suddenly, I had a strong feeling that Endo was down with us, looking up at the deck just as we were . . . .

Take care of yourself . . . .

For U . . . . A Dirge

Early leaves weep on the willows by the moat
Wrapped in misty rain, beneath a smiling sky

The water lies clear-cut and still
Seeking a dirge in my heart

All farewells made without fuss
All grief wiped away without fuss

As though a blessing still loomed faint in the distance,
    I will walk away;
Now is the time for me to disappear into the invisible,
    to the eternity beyond.

translated by John Bester

Katsuzō Oda

Human Ashes

August 6th, 1945, morning:

ON the streets going toward Eba from the Yokogawa Station in Hiroshima, the air was thick with dust. Houses and shops, their occupants forced to evacuate, were being torn down to make a firebreak and there was such a litter of broken tiles and chunks of plaster wall scattered over the street that it all but blocked the progress of the streetcar. Disordered files of people passed ceaselessly back and forth along the street, probably a party of volunteer workers who had been dispatched to help out with the demolition of the buildings.

The streetcar, forced to slow its pace, moved ahead almost at the same speed as the columns of people in the street, running alongside them. Wholly by chance, I noticed one of my Hiroshima aunts among the jostling crowd.

Though I had been introduced to all my Hiroshima relatives, I had never even spoken a word to this aunt—she was really hardly more to me than a stranger. But when her listless-looking face suddenly came into view right below the window of the streetcar, I was so startled I very nearly shouted out her name. In the end, though, seeing her there among a group of people I didn't even know, I couldn't get up nerve enough to call to her.

Little by little the figure of my aunt, which had appeared so vividly and unexpectedly, receded into the distance. I strained my eyes to keep sight of her dwindling form, but before long she disappeared from view in the chalky air and the press of people. A cold sweat remained in my palms where I had clenched my hands into tense fists.

My parents and I, forced to evacuate Osaka because of the bombings, had recently moved in with relatives living in the countryside near Hiroshima, and the move had brought drastic changes in my life. I was now obliged to spend about two hours every morning traveling into town to school, and every day was passed among surroundings that were utterly new to me. And, as in the case of the aunt I had just caught sight of, I could not seem to open up and make friends with any of my newfound Hiroshima relatives.

This morning the streetcar was more crowded than ever. It was shortly after I had seen my aunt that I first noticed the soldier in khaki uniform standing off to one side behind me. Looking at his face, I could see beads of glistening sweat running down his ruddy forehead and cheeks. Sweat not only bathed his face but soaked his shirt from the collar insignia all the way down to the middle of his chest, turning it a dark color. I could tell at once he was a student at the army prep school. He stood stiff as a pole in his uniform, not swaying an inch with the motion of the trolley.

I turned away and then after a while looked back at his bright eyes. Outside of a faint sound made by his breathing, he was utterly still and silent. The smell of my own sweat and the waves of heat I could feel coming to me from the body of the young soldier suddenly roused in me a feeling of vague excitement.

My one dream at that time was to shoulder a gun and go off to battle. In particular, all during the past month, the midmonth of summer, my head had been constantly filled with tragic thoughts of the kamikaze pilots going off to their death.

At the same time, since I was just entering puberty, quite different types of thoughts, the sudden stirrings of sexual awakening, were beginning to seek an outlet. Both sets of thoughts, however, remained silent and unexpressed in the inner depths of my being. In Hiroshima, a place that was still strange to me, I was intensely lonely and isolated.

The incident that occurred next in the streetcar was simplicity itself. The cause was probably some happening too trifling to warrant notice. But the little dispute that ensued quickly generated an atmosphere of ugly and unrelenting belligerence. Some students began punching a workman.

"Bastard! Do you want your face pushed in?"

The harsh, threatening voices of the students lashed out over the heads of the other passengers.

"What do you mean, dummy! I never pushed you!"

The argument was over who had stepped on whose foot. Then the mounting anger suddenly went to their heads and one party or other began hitting out.

I knew the students by sight. We often rode the same trolley in the morning. I could tell from their collar insignia that they were a class ahead of me. And I was also familiar with the kind of trouble that their bunch were likely to stir up within the narrow confines of the streetcar. They regularly terrorized the meek conductor so that he was too frightened to collect their fares, or shoved their way rudely into the crowd of passengers, shouting in affected voices, "Look at the clams with their mouths hanging open!", joking and carrying on as though they were the only ones on the streetcar.

When the streetcar came to a stop, the students dragged the workman down onto the tracks and began grappling with him. But the workman was shrewd enough to know he had no chance against so many opponents. Then all of a sudden someone in a khaki uniform was standing defiantly in the midst of the group. It was the student from the army prep school. He made no sound at all, and that seemed to have a particularly potent effect. Then with his heavy military boot he kicked the students in the stomach and sent them scattering. The workman stood for a moment gaping at the sudden interloper, but when he saw it was a soldier in uniform, he fled in panic to the other side of the tracks.

The students at first looked as though they would put up some resistance but, perhaps intimidated by the peculiarly silent assault of the soldier, they spat angrily and turned on their heels.

The prep school student did not get back on the streetcar. And when he turned his back and began walking away, as though to bring down the curtain on a scene from a play, a siren sounded. It was the usual warning of an air raid.

7:30 *a.m.*

The roll call of students assigned to work duty was held in the open ground in front of the factory. I don't remember exactly what the sky was like at the time. I'm certain there was no bright sunlight, but just what sort of cloud formation covered the sky I couldn't say.

After solemnly reciting the Imperial Rescript to Military Personnel, the students, with the upperclassmen in the lead, proceeded to their respective workshops. I think it was at that time that I heard, somewhere behind my back, the signal informing us that the air raid warning had been lifted.

I was assigned to duty in the Second Machine Shop. Inside the dimly lit workshop the students were subjected to a second roll call. The man who carried this out was a foreman, a former worker who had something wrong with his leg. Standing so that his wiry body bent over backwards, he invariably treated us to the same speech every morning. The lenses of his glasses were so thick that it was impossible to tell which way his eyes were looking. The effect brought to mind the big round compound eyes of an insect.

The students called him Dragonfly and made fun of him behind his back. When I first heard the nickname, I couldn't help admiring the person who thought it up. Because that's exactly what he looked like, forever circling round and round the workshop.

After the foreman had finished his customary admonitory address and the students were preparing to go to their stations, I noticed someone hiding in the darkness beside the pool of water where logs were floated. I had to pass right by there in order to get to my own station, and as I did so, I guessed in an instant who it must be.

"Oyamada!" I could hear someone calling my name in a low, wavery voice. Just as I thought—it was Ichikawa. He was in the same class as me but a little older.

"I'm going to my country place," he said, his dark brown lips moving rapidly, and the meaningful stare he gave me indicated that I was to take care of things afterward.

"All right," I replied obediently. But Ichikawa, not even waiting to make sure of my answer, had already scampered monkey-like across the floor and disappeared outside.

His "country place" was the warehouse. There there were numerous wooden barrels stacked in tall piles, each one big enough for a person to crawl into.

Ichikawa was a bad character. But he had never bullied me out of money or belongings the way he did the other students in the class. On the contrary, his attitude somehow suggested that he was trying to look out for me because I was all alone. So if I had to choose, I'd say I felt more friendly toward Ichikawa, even though the bad things he did scared me, than I did toward the other students in the class who pretended to be so good but at heart were so mean.

Moving among the hum of motors, I stared at Ichikawa's

figure as he hurried in the direction of the warehouse. Soon, in the darkness of a barrel, he would be sucking on an illicit piece of candy—its manufacture was prohibited because of the sugar shortage—and masturbating happily.

I don't know just how much time passed after that, but I was cleaning up some bits of sawed-off board from the floor in the vicinity of one of the upperclassmen when he called my name.

"Oyamada!"

"Yes?"

"Have you seen Ichikawa?"

"Yes. Today is his turn to act as orderly." The lie popped right out of my mouth.

"Huh?" said the upperclassman in a suspicious tone. Evidently unwilling to accept my explanation, he went on to say something more, but his words were drowned by the hum of the motor and I couldn't catch them. As a matter of fact, I had already begun sidling away from him. If he should start cross-examining me, I was not sure I could keep up the deception.

I went and sat down under the plate of the forging press, wedging myself into place under it. The cold musty smell of machine oil struck my nostrils. Suddenly I thought of Ichikawa. I envied him his uninhibited approach to sex. In a part of my own body too I could feel irrepressible sexual desires beginning to well up.

"Oyamada!" I heard the upperclassman calling me. Apparently he had been calling my name for some time. Hurriedly I started to move out from under the press.

To say that I saw it at that instant is not quite accurate. The phenomenon that occurred at that instant registered on my eyeballs, but I had no way of knowing what it was. And whatever it was, it came and went with extraordinary speed. At first I thought it was something I had dreamed.

The open space in front of the factory that was visible beyond the glass window was filled with flames. But it was not that the ground was on fire and sending up flames. So I suppose I'd have to say that the flames were spewed down from the sky and were licking at the earth.

But then with astonishing speed the instant came to an end and reality returned. Only it was a kind of stunned reality, full of terrible contradictions.

Darkness was enveloping everything in front of my eyes, but at the same time I could perceive that the heavy beam that supported the roof of the workshop was lying on the ground right by my feet. The upperclassman who had been calling my name was standing in a stupor beside it. He was staring with a look of amazement at the blood spurting out of his shoulder where the arm joined it. His arm dangled limply.

As I finally began to take in the scene around me, the first words that came to my mind were, "Am I going to die in a place like this?" As yet, though, there was no sense of fear in the thought. Only a kind of astonishment. The darkness that had surrounded me probably lasted only for a moment, as did the roaring noise over my head, though I don't actually remember hearing the roar.

When the scene in front of me had brightened a little, I commenced instinctively to move around. I was crawling and searching for some way out of the tangle of machinery, disengaged machine belts and debris of smashed-in roof that covered me. Nearby I could see a triangular window. The window had originally been square but it had been completely blown out, leaving only the twisted frame.

I managed to make my way outside. Everything was quiet and there was no one around. But as I started to run, I saw someone's head sticking out right beside the narrow entrance. It was Dragonfly. His wings and body had been crushed under a thick beam and just his head, mixed with some kind of white substance, was poking out. Bloody vomit had come out of his mouth and he was dead.

I ran without stopping till I reached the open space in front of the factory. There everyone was running around. I noticed that the commotion was making little ripples on the stagnant gray pond where water was stored for fire fighting. The door of the air-raid shelter had been blown off and I could see smoke, apparently from burning paraffin, pouring out and ascending in a column. A hot wind was blowing from somewhere and a strange heaviness in the air seemed to envelop me. At that moment terror for the first time took violent hold of my mind. Waves of nausea swept over me as I ran toward the factory gate.

Here and there on the ground, orange flames were leaping up from pieces of shattered buildings. There were so many fires I thought someone must have set them deliberately. In the sky directly overhead, dark, low lying masses of air flowed by, but in the direction of the harbor the sky was clear blue.

Needless to say, neither I nor anyone else had the slightest idea what had brought about this sudden freakish event.

As I came running out the factory gate, I saw that Second Lieutenant Yamane, the military officer attached to our school, had jumped into the river that ran in front of the factory and was shouting something.

"Watch out! It's a naval bombardment! Wet yourselves down!" I heard him calling.

Two or three students like frightened frogs had followed the lieutenant's lead and jumped into the river. The lieutenant was standing near the shore, pointing at me and shouting again. But I held back, not because I couldn't swim, but because it looked like such an absurd thing to do in the middle of the day.

Then I heard shouts like a cry for help from the direction of the factory office. "The teacher's dead!"

I didn't know who the teacher was but, as though pulled on by the cries, I hurried toward the office. What I saw there was almost too horrible to believe. The teacher was Mr. Naka-yama, and he may still have been alive. A big sliver of glass was sticking into his throat and blood was shooting out in great spurts and splashing down over his chest.

I felt the ground open under me and my legs, suddenly numb, seemed to be sinking into it. What in the world kind of day *was* this! We hadn't heard a single bomb drop, we hadn't seen a trace of an enemy plane. The sky had been perfectly peace-ful . . . .

I was in love with Mr. Nakayama in a vague way, though I had never said or done the slightest thing to show it. I had visited his house twice. His wife, like Mr. Nakayama himself, was a kindhearted person and she was also very beautiful. But on those occasions too I had been as inarticulate as usual. From first to last, the love I felt for Mr. Nakayama and his wife remained concealed by shyness and hesitation. Now, however, whatever mild feelings of affection I may have felt were so abruptly altered by what I saw that it was all I could do to keep from trying to spit them out in the violent waves of nausea that gripped me.

"Fall in!" It was Lieutenant Yamane, who had now climbed up on the embankment, waving his arms and bellowing. He seemed somewhat deranged and his frenzied shouts resembled the outcries of a suddenly frightened animal. Needless to say, they made no sense at all.

What happened next was wholly contrary to the lieutenant's expectations. The students, far from obeying his order to fall in, wheeled around and began running in the opposite direc-tion. To the lieutenant, whose authority until now had never for an instant been challenged, it must have seemed an incredi-ble sight. This sudden change in the attitude of the students was an insult not to be endured. More frantic than ever, he hopped up and down, flailing his arms and shouting. But nobody looked in his direction.

I went back to the factory, not running this time. I had decided to go out the rear gate. The factory was totally wrecked, some parts of it still burning, others by now burned out.

When I reached the warehouse, I could see that the barrels stacked inside were in total disorder, with some of them crushed flat. Hardly any retained their original shape—the rest had lost their bottom or been broken apart. Among the barrels there was something that looked like blood and a foot sticking out. I halted a minute and looked at the dirty foot but didn't try to find out if it was Ichikawa's. At that point I knew it would be wasted effort.

When I arrived at the rear entrance, the situation was quite different from that in the factory. Here the indistinct buzz of living beings that I had heard from a distance shaped itself into actual human voices calling back and forth. As yet there was no sense of panic. Among the people passing by me I even spotted smiling faces. Nearly all the people had burned clothing and they walked along in files like ants.

Had they been burned by the flames from the sky? I wondered. I was convinced then that what I had seen in that moment in the factory had indeed been some kind of "fire from heaven."

Since I knew so little about the geography of the city, I decided to walk in the direction of the green hills I could see in the distance.

The overhead wires that the trolley cars ran on were plastered all over the streets like cobwebs and people with bare feet were stepping over them. Some brown-colored animals—whether dogs or cats I couldn't tell—lay tumbled by the road.

Everything has been burned! I thought. Everything had a brownish color. Even the asphalt on the street had turned the color of an old frying pan.

"Which way is Ujina?" someone asked. But I didn't know where Ujina was.

"Over that way?" asked the person, pointing to the sky. His eyes were hollow and unfocussed. It was one of the group of rowdy students I had seen on the streetcar that morning. I was so startled at the coincidence I didn't think to answer.

"Stupid! Don't you know?" the student exclaimed, his lips twisting in irritation. Then he began to walk on, poised as though he were gazing at the sky. I was watching from behind when he abruptly fell over in the road. Drops of dark blood dripped from the back of his head and gray brain matter was oozing out. I stared apathetically and then, as though it were nothing, walked on.

When I came out along the Temma River, I saw many more people than I had before; they were lying down by the riverside, terribly still. Their clothing too was charred and blackened and they had to hold it in place. I was especially struck by the peculiar way the women's hair had shriveled.

Hurriedly I began feeling all over my own body to make certain I was all right. I suddenly felt uneasy, wondering if perhaps all the time I had been fleeing this far my brains had been sticking out the back of my head like the student's, or if I had a hole in my back that I somehow hadn't noticed.

Most of the people I saw did in fact have injuries somewhere on their bodies. And what was really odd, wherever their skin was exposed, it didn't look like ordinary skin at all, but had a pale pink color. It was a long time later I learned that the color was caused by burns.

The crowd gradually swelled in number. Under the circumstances, no one seemed to want to move on his own. This was particularly evident with the women and children, who would fall in behind anyone, even a stranger, and walk along. I fell into line and began walking with the others because I decided I wanted to cross the bridge that I could see some distance up the river.

As we neared the approach to the bridge, however, the congestion began to get much worse. The narrow road running along the embankment seethed with waves of people pushing now in one direction, now in another, the air thick with the clamor of their voices and the foul smell of charred things.

Below the embankment I could see a woman holding a baby to her breast and covering her mouth with a dirty towel. Clearly she was no longer in her right mind. She stared at me with frightening eyes and then, as though pleading for help, shook her head vigorously. Finally she picked up some small stones and threw them at the people passing nearby.

We could hear a roar from the black smoke streaming up from the downtown area, and the voices coming from the columns of ragged people, continually calling out a babble of names to no one in particular, echoed across the broad surface of the river.

Rice paddies flanked both sides of the river, their green so intense it dazzled the eye. There I saw a naked woman, so badly burned she had fallen to the ground, a small child standing close beside her, apparently calling to its mother. No, it was not just one woman who had collapsed from burns. There were dozens of people there, struggling painfully to reach the water of the river.

I could hear gasping voices calling out repeatedly, complaining of the heat or begging for water. The people lying in the fields tried to grab hold of the feet of the uninjured persons who were passing by, but no one stopped to listen to them.

It was in that vicinity that the black rain fell on us. The big drops that all at once began pelting down utterly dumbfounded the people on the road. There was nothing that looked like an ordinary cloud in the sky, and yet from the black smoke streaming over our heads a heavy rain was falling. As we watched, the roads and fields turned dark with it.

Now what's happening! we thought. All eyes turned uneasily

toward the sky, and then we looked at each other in perplexity. There was no doubt about it—the rain was black with some sort of dirt or contamination.

At that moment, a kind of panic began to well up from somewhere in the crowd, and first one voice and then another started passing along the message: "It's gasoline! The Americans are dumping gasoline on us!"

To the people who had managed to escape the earlier flames, this was enough to plunge them once more into frenzies of terror. These people in recent months had been repeatedly subjected to stories of the enemy's ruthless cruelties, and there was probably not a soul among them who doubted the truth of what the voices were saying. They were certain that at the touch of a match their bodies would be enveloped in gasoline flames and there would be no way to escape.

A shudder of fear ran through the crowd. I felt a sharp blow from somewhere and fell to my knees. My heart seemed about to stop beating and a terrible pressure bore down on me, as though something were clamped over my ears.

But the rain let up almost immediately. I brought my arm up to my lips and tasted the drops of rain on it. They had no particular taste. Though I didn't know what gasoline tasted like, I went on tasting the drops again and again. I couldn't be sure, but it certainly didn't seem to be gasoline.

The confusion around me, however, showed no signs of abating. Now and then I could hear women screaming or children wailing.

Drawing aside a little, I looked at the scene and at that point decided to separate from the crowd. If I walked in the direction of the hills, something would work out. To go on moving with a mass of people like this seemed more dangerous than striking out on my own. Fortunately, the sense of isolation that was so constant a part of me gave me the courage to do so. I noticed that by now the people lying by the river had become very still again. Whether gasoline or real rain, the cool substance that had fallen from the sky had evidently given some relief to their fevered bodies.

Passing through the mist that hung over the surface of the river, I crossed a bridge whose name I didn't know. After I had also crossed the main railway line running east and west and made my way to the foot of the green hills, I turned and for the first time looked back at the city. I could see that the center of the fire was rather a long way off. And I also realized that, after encountering that strange instant in the factory at Eba, the route by which I had fled had fortunately made a wide detour around the fire. Quietly the realization came to me that I had escaped.

I was not the only one with that thought. Here, where the road lifted up into the hills, a number of other people were gazing far off at the burning city, doubtless thinking the same thing.

The narrow country road had been badly damaged, perhaps by the sudden downpour of rain that had fallen. It looked as though something had just recently been dragged over it, leaving spots where the reddish earth was newly exposed.

Going on a little farther, I spotted a red cross flag among a grove of trees. I could see some kind of tent enclosure as well. In contrast to the chaos of the morning, this spot seemed to preserve something of the kind of calm and order that had prevailed until today.

I had no sooner set foot in the grove, however, when I saw that there were countless blackened, ash-covered human forms lying about in the thickets of bamboo. For a second I doubted my eyes. I doubted my ears too, for the low, droning voices were like none I had ever heard. If human flesh is burned through and through, will it really fall apart like this? Oil and sweat, along with streams of fresh blood, flowed from the bodies, and the place was black with swarming flies. How could I have been so mistaken as to take this for a place of calm and order?

"Excuse me—you're a student, aren't you?" said a woman's voice. The woman was sitting on the ground. She looked to be about my mother's age.

"Are you a student in the First Middle School or the Second Middle School?" she asked.

Despite the disheveled hair and pale, trembling lips, she appeared, like me, to have escaped injury. But what kind of turmoil was going on inside her? Her wide staring eyes seemed abnormally dry, her arms hung limply by her side, and she pulled off tufts of grass and crushed them in her fist.

"I'm not at either," I replied. It was the first time I had spoken and my voice sounded hoarse. "I'm at Sanyō Middle School."

"Sanyō," the woman parroted. "You see, you never know when or what kind of air raid there's going to be. So all the members of my family agreed that if we should ever get separated, we'd meet here at this hill," she continued.

"What school is your son in?" I asked.

"Second Middle."

I made no comment.

"You didn't see any students from Second Middle?"

I shook my head.

The woman's shoulders slumped with disappointment. I suppose she had been going around asking everyone the same sort of question.

"If only my boy got away all right the way you did . . . ." Her voice was tinged with despair and hopeless longing.

The woman rose unsteadily to her feet and pointed at the other people. "Just look at that!" she said. "How could they do anything so ghastly! These people are all burned completely black . . . . you don't know what a job I had bringing them this far!"

Though the woman was talking to me, she seemed to ignore my existence entirely. Turning her back, she went on speaking. "Still, those who got this far before they died are lucky. What about the ones who were pinned under their houses and couldn't get out at all!"

Suddenly the woman turned her head and stared at me. Her eyes were drawn tight with emotion. "If they do dreadful things like this, God is going to get really angry!"

For an instant I flinched, as though her words had struck me in the chest. Up to that moment I hadn't really thought carefully about what had happened. Certainly the word "God" had not occurred to me. It just seemed as though everything had become smothered in ashes and terror, that was all. Now if she was prepared to denounce it as the tyranny of human beings who had no fear of God, then her understanding must be much more profound than mine. I didn't know what to make of her words or how to answer them.

Summing up all my strength, I said, "I think the people at Second Middle will be all right." The fact that the students of Second Middle had been assigned to duty at a factory much farther down near the mouth of the river from us at Eba for the moment eluded my mind.

But my words seemed to have no effect. The woman's eyes abruptly overflowed with tears and she sank down weeping. Her thin, long-drawn-out wails rose from among the clumps of grass as though they would never end.

Then I noticed there was a white badge hanging from the cord of her *mompe* work trousers with the words "volunteer worker" inked on it in black letters. The label "volunteer worker" was to be seen practically everywhere in Japan at that time—there was certainly nothing unusual about it. Young or old, man or woman, every day people were being pressed into service for some sort of work or other. This woman too had no doubt been called out for volunteer duty and had had to leave her home.

At that moment an image flashed into my mind. It was the figure of the aunt I had seen that morning and had completely forgotten about until now. She appeared as vividly as though she were passing right before my eyes. She had covered her head with a light towel to keep off the sun and of course was wearing *mompe* trousers, and on her feet were canvas shoes of the type elementary school children wear—details such as these I could recall without difficulty. I even recalled that on her arm was a badge marked "volunteer worker" like the one this woman had.

Then it occurred to me that this woman might have been in the same jostling column of workers as my aunt this morning. I laid my hand on her shoulder as she hunched over crying and shook her gently. "Excuse me, lady," I said, and leaned down to speak into her ear. But in answer she only shook her head from side to side, and in the end never even looked up.

The thought came to me that just possibly my aunt had fled from the city and was right here on this hill. If she had escaped, there was a possibility that here, among all this frantic, heated confusion, I might actually come face to face with one of my own blood kin. The hope of such an encounter seized hold of my mind with uncanny vigor. To meet my aunt—that would be to meet the most reliable witness there could be to the reality of this day of destruction that had suddenly come crashing down on us, someone who had gone through it all just as I had. I had completely forgotten that I had never spoken a word to my aunt and was on anything but familiar terms with her.

I walked over the trampled stalks of summer grass and approached the tent. Inside, a soldier who looked like a medical corpsman was busy conferring with representatives from town assemblies and neighborhood organizations and there seemed to be no chance to break in on the conversation. I decided instead to stop the first person I happened to meet and ask if there was any news of the party of volunteer workers I had seen this morning.

Fortunately the first man I approached turned out to be of an obliging nature. "Sir, there's something I'd like to ask you," I said, raising my hand in a salute, as was the custom at the time.

"Yes?"

"I wonder if that group of volunteer workers down around Dobashi are all right?"

"Oh—those people." He was still in a state of agitation, it appeared, and spoke in a very loud voice. "Ah—I'm afraid none of them got out of it. All dead. You see, they were right out in the street. Had no protection at all."

After a moment, he asked, "Was there somebody you know in the party?"

"My aunt."

"Your aunt? Well now, I'm very sorry." The bridge of the man's nose was covered with wrinkles as he spoke. "What happened, you see—the enemy planes flew in a direct line right over Hiroshima. Dropped bombs all over. And not the kind of bombs they've been dropping up to now. Bombs that exploded right in midair and burned everything completely!" He spoke in a tone that might almost have been called hearty, gesturing again and again with his hands to show how the enemy planes had dropped their bombs.

That was the first time I had heard a coherent account of the enemy raid. I couldn't tell whether this man had actually witnessed the raid, but there seemed nothing to do but believe his words, particularly when he spoke with such assurance. I wondered, however, if the Dobashi work party had in fact been entirely wiped out the way he said. After all, I had just en-countered a woman who might well have been a member of the party and she had managed to survive. There was no proof one way or the other.

"Thank you very much," I said, turning to go.

"You don't seem to be hurt," he called after me. "That's splendid, just splendid! Now you better get along home."

I walked through the grove of trees, which sheltered a small, dilapidated Shinto shrine, and out into an open space. There I could see a jumble of bodies lying on the ground. Life had not yet left them entirely, though most were clearly on the verge of death. As though to wall them in, crowds of living persons had gathered around. I stepped over the bodies of the dying— there was no other way to go about it—and, amid the sound of their moans, searched carefully back and forth. I wondered at myself for behaving so brazenly, like a person possessed; and yet I could not resist the impulse to go on hunting for my aunt.

The stench that hovered over the place seemed to drive out all thought and leave me with an indescribable feeling of irritation. At some point one of my gaiters came undone, though apparently quite a time passed before I noticed it.

I walked up the steps of the little shrine and gazed around. It looked as though Death had suddenly broken through the dam and come wildly roaring down upon the living, leaving this scene of wreckage behind. And for all I knew, my aunt might be among those who had been swept up and deposited here.

Somehow, however, the sight did not seem sad. I saw it as an opportunity to observe in detail the process by which human beings die. It awoke in me a sense of great wonderment, even of curiosity.

I noticed that the grove was beginning to darken with the onset of evening. The trees, the shrine, the blackened human beings seemed blurry and far away, as though a film had covered my eyes. I realized I had had nothing to eat since early morning. But my stomach did not feel empty. It felt as though it were stuck up against my back, held there by a dull nausea that refused to go away.

I was tired. But I did not stop searching back and forth over the area. I kept thinking what it would be like to come face to face with my aunt and find she was all right.

Sometime or other, I came out on a slope behind the shrine. Here too there was a tent with a mark identifying it as a first-aid station. But there was no sign of a doctor administering relief—only a noisy, milling crowd of people gathered around to receive rations of crackers.

I stood absently watching the proceedings. A number of soldiers pushed past me, jolting my shoulder and barking at me to get out of the way. They were nearly naked and were daubing some uncommonly evil-smelling oily substance on the spots where they were burned.

My eyes all at once came to rest on a woman who, like me, seemed to be standing in a daze. She was wearing darkish *mompe*, and the upper part of her body was barely covered by a flimsy white chemise. A charred fire-protection hood hung from her neck, apparently just as she had tied it, and her thin fingers gripped its tattered edge. When she turned so I could see the profile of her face in the dim light under the trees, a cry of astonishment rang through my head. My knees seemed to give way and I could feel the hot blood rushing to my head. "It's the wife of our teacher, Mr. Nakayama!" I exclaimed under my breath.

A feeling of confusion seized me. She was near enough so that if I called in a loud voice she would surely turn and look in my direction. But in the brief instant while I hesitated whether to call her or not, she hurried off and disappeared into the throng of people in front of the tent.

On the bare flesh of one shoulder, she had a blister from a burn that sagged as though it were about to burst at any moment, and a bloodstained towel was wrapped around her narrow waist.

I set off after her. It was just as a new group of persons moved into place to receive their ration of crackers and there was a certain amount of confusion. The shouts of the soldier doling out the crackers, which were intended to restore order, had little effect. Shoved and jostled by one person after another, the woman wormed her way in among the crowd.

I intended to keep following the woman, but I was caught among half naked people with painfully inflamed skin and I could no longer move. Then someone shouted "Children have to wait their turn!" and began pulling me by the back of the neck.

I started to say "I'm not in line—I'm looking for someone!", but at that moment the person yanked with all his strength and I was dragged to one side and thrown down on the grass.

I hit my head against a pine tree, but although I felt a slight numbness and a dull ache, I got to my feet immediately. In the end, though, I was never able to catch sight of the woman again.

I wondered if I was suffering from some kind of illusion. For all I knew in my feverish search for my aunt I had seen someone who looked a good deal like Mr. Nakayama's wife and mistaken her for the real person.

By the time the turmoil in front of the tent had died down, the long summer day was at last drawing to a close. My leaden feet dragging, I left the spot.

When I returned to the front of the shrine, I could see, beyond the dark shapes of the trees, the gleam of fires where corpses were being cremated. As time passed, the heartlessness of the sight began to press down like a great weight on my mind and a choking loneliness gripped my chest.

Wedged in between people I did not know, I sat huddled under an awning that had been rigged among the trees. The people around me stared at the flames of the burning pyres as they talked back and forth in low voices.

With nightfall many of the people had drifted away, but there were still quite a few remaining who apparently intended to spend the night there.

Perhaps from sheer exhaustion, I no longer felt like doing anything at all. I tore off blades of grass and chewed them up, tasting the sour, pungent juice, and thought how my mother and the others would be worrying about me and waiting anxiously for my return. Soon after, I fell into a deep sleep.

Dim memories of nightmares I used to have as a child when I was running a high fever came to life again, and pale human faces passed before my eyes, appearing and disappearing, disappearing and appearing in the midst of flames, jets of spurting blood and black smoke.

I couldn't remember how I happened to be sleeping there, but with morning I woke suddenly to find the middle school uniform I was wearing damp and heavy with dew.

How short the night had been! I got to my feet as soon as I woke and, still surprised to think I could have spent a whole night in such a place, looked around.

The dazzling rays of the summer morning sun poured through the grove of trees surrounding the shrine. It was as though a huge zebra were bending its head and peering in at the shrine. Under the trees a scattering of people still lay sleeping quietly.

The funeral fires of the night before had gone out, and I could see that all that remained was white smoke and white ashes—human ashes.

translated by Burton Watson

Yōko Ōta

Fireflies

I

ALTHOUGH I had visited the site the previous morning, I went again the next afternoon to see the stone walls of the ruined castle as they stood facing each other like the sleeves on a kimono.

Whether they used to be one of the castle gates or part of the solid rampart, I couldn't tell, since only the ruins remained. The obvious assumption was that, unrealistic as it seemed, a section of the otherwise destroyed rampart still stood there.

It was past noon on a June day. I was standing between the two tall stone walls. The earth under my feet was shadowed as in a valley. The wall that I was facing appeared grotesque and on fire whenever I went back to see it. The surface of each stone in the wall, big and small alike, was burning in colors of brown, rusty vermilion and bright red. Summer grass was growing out of the cracks. Yellow flowers were blooming on the grass tips.

There was enough room for people to walk on the top of the wall. The grass and its flowers spread over the whole top. To me this giant wall seemed to brim with a kind of impressive beauty. One of the artists from Tokyo had been struck with the idea of engraving a poem in these burned stones. He wanted to carve the words written by a poet who had killed himself. I understood his intention well enough, and yet I knew about the nightmares that this place had seen.

I had never met the poet Tamiki Hara, but I had read the words written from his soul in "Requiem".

—Never live for yourself. Live only for the grief of the dead. I told myself again and again.—

—Pierce my body, Oh, Grief! Pierce my body, Countless Griefs!—

Several people came from Tokyo to select a place for a monument with Tamiki Hara's poetry engraved on it. I looked at a few places with them because, luckily or not, I had come to Hiroshima a couple of days before then. They all liked the radiation-burned stone wall, but I didn't. Only Tamiki Hara and I, with the eyes and souls we had in common, should be able to see the colors of the stone wall in the castle site. The eyes and souls of the visitors from Tokyo, who had never experienced the intense light of radiation, were different from ours.

To me the stones seemed to burn like balls of flame: Or I thought that the stones, retaining the rays of the midday sun, were actually hot. As I had done many times before, I passed my hand over the stone surfaces, feeling for some heat. They weren't hot, but there was a feeling of brittleness, as if they would soon crumble into fragments. The other sleeve of wall across the way, which had received the full force of the light of the bomb streaming down from the central part of the city, was burned a mottled shade of red. But the part of the wall where the surface had not been exposed to the direct light was not red. Rather, it seemed to be deteriorated and to have taken on the calm gray of a fossil. There was sand spilling out of its broken surface.

The wall was one and a half meters thick. If it had been a human body, it would have been burned up. I couldn't forget the scenes in which human faces had been burned exactly like this. I thought that the Tamiki Hara poetry monument, if erected here, might take on the same flaming color as the wall. Perhaps it was merely a morbid reaction. Come to think of it, wherever I happened to be in Hiroshima, although seven years had passed since the bombing, my eyes seemed to see only masses of fire and blood everywhere.

The shadow of dusk began to cover part of the stone walls. Evening clouds changed their shapes moment by moment. I thought about the poet who had had to take his own life and tried to relate his death to my own life and death. That was why I stood by the walls. But I had stood there too long, I realized, and I left. The place was deserted. By the moat was a slender willow tree, looking picturesque in its setting. It had caught my eye from the beginning, and I went and crouched down under it, because it looked like a good spot from which to sketch the walls. I put my drawing pad on my knees and opened it. I was not good at drawing, but I somehow managed to catch the shape of each stone in the walls. And then I started writing about the colors of the stones, the green grass, and the small yellow flowers. Two men came along. I saw the light of a cigarette. The men were carrying shovels on their shoulders.

They were probably workmen on their way back from cleaning up after the athletic exposition that had been held on the grounds of the castle site. The men squatted down at the edge of the moat and looked at me writing on my pad. Then they walked past me without a word. After they had passed, one of them turned around and asked inquiringly, "Lady?"—with a tone of sweetness—"what are you thinking about so seriously?"

The other man turned back, too, after walking a little way past me.

"Good evening," he said slowly, as if suddenly remembering the expression. I nearly burst out laughing.

"Good evening," I replied to their backs.

They both stopped and turned around again. Then they said from a distance, "You're not going to jump in the moat, are you? Leave a note behind? You're not going to kill yourself?"

"No, I'm not going to kill myself!"

The men walked away laughing. I had no intention of dying the way Tamiki Hara did. And yet, a lurking sense of death was always around me. I was trying to live, but on the other hand there was always the danger of death.

The sun was about to set. The stone walls were sinking into darkness. And yet I was able to make out each stone clearly, as if it were a living being.

I started back toward the makeshift shacks at the former military training ground, which was four or five streets from the downtown area. Turning my back on the stone walls, I began walking. It seemed as though those stone cliffs, turning into flames, were collapsing behind me. The feeling was not a false one. To me that was the ultimate truth.

2

While in Hiroshima, I was staying at my youngest sister Teiko's house. The place she lived in was not what you would normally call a "house". I didn't know the right word for it —a shack, a barrack, some kind of little living unit appropriate to this devastated city.

I understood that it was a makeshift affair, and yet it was not only for temporary use because my sister had been living there for seven years since the war. And it didn't seem as though she was planning to move into a real house.

"Just once more in my lifetime I'd like to live in a house with running water," Teiko said. She was thirty-one years old.

"Don't sound so discouraged. Aren't there a lot of people who have moved out of these shacks and built new houses somewhere else?"

"No, almost none."

"Nobody? There are so many people here."

"I've never heard of it happening."

When the city was reduced to rubble, not a single house was left standing. The makeshift shacks were erected on the training ground, which was still strewn with the bones of numberless soldiers who had been burned to death there. It was strange to think of the shacks going up, a thousand of them in one corner of the training ground, built by the city for the relief of the survivors.

The facilities should have been able to house everybody, since the number of survivors was not that great. But because all the older houses had been destroyed, and because repatriates from abroad and discharged soldiers were pouring into the city, the shacks were soon filled up. Teiko, her husband, a junior high teacher, and her two-year-old daughter had managed to move into one of the units. That was at the end of 1946. The shack had two rooms, one designed to be floored with six tatami mats, the other with three mats. But at first the rooms were not even floored with mats because there were too many thieves and beggers around to make off with them. Teiko and her husband Soichi, with their little daughter tied onto her back, picked their way along a small path across the desolate army field, the cold wind sweeping over them, to go to the city housing office to pick up their tatami mats. Because all the huts were built to standardized dimensions, it didn't make any difference which mats and fixtures Teiko and Soichi picked out. They took nine tatami mats and a couple of wooden and glass doors and carried them back on their shoulders. None of the poorly-made tatami mats and doors fitted properly, so they had to wedge and stuff them into place as best they could.

There was no ceiling. The unfinished logs that served as beams formed a triangle that was open to view. Morning sunlight found its way between the wooden beams into the room. Here and there I could see the heads of nails and I felt as though I was lying in a log cabin in the mountains. There was a tiny toilet at the end of the open veranda. It looked like something built for children—you could imagine it pushing away any grownup who tried to use it. Inside were two rough boards placed over a shallow pot which was fully exposed to view.

And yet these were not slum dwellings. They were all separate units, with spaces in between, and there were rows and rows of them like so many long walls. No matter how harsh the circumstances, people can hardly be expected to put up with communal living for long. Here the occupants at least had their separate little roosts where they could guard their own particular secrets from one another. The lines and lines of small shacks were proof of this.

There was only one source of water for the occupants of the huts in Teiko's row and those opposite them. There had been a water outlet at the Army horse stables, but the pipe had been broken in the bombing. Until the water pipe was repaired, all the families in all one thousand shacks had gone all the way to Sakancho to get water, walking across the training grounds and over Aioi Bridge, right through the area where the bomb had burst. Now, however, the water pipe at the stables had been repaired, and Teiko and the others went back and forth from morning to night to draw water there, carrying their house keys in hand.

One rainy night I came back late. Since there was no real entrance, I could come into the hut from either the front or the back as I pleased. When I called out to Teiko from the back door, I heard someone inside pulling out a nail. Teiko looked at me with her large dark eyes. The corners of her mouth were scarred with keloid marks that stood out like welts. One step in from the outside was the three-mat living room. After I had changed into some dry clothes and sat down at the dilapidated table, my eyes were drawn to a number of slugs creeping around. Teiko put a light supper on the table and sat down across from me to pour the tea.

"Terrible slugs!" I said.

"Yes. We're trying to get rid of them but they just keep coming."

Soichi had rigged a clothes closet in one corner of the room. It didn't have a door but was hung with a tattered curtain. There was a small can full of thick salt water behind the curtain. Teiko took it out and, with a pair of cheap chopsticks, picked up the slugs and dropped them in the can one by one. It gave me a creepy feeling. The slugs slithered around in droves at the base of the sliding paper doors, which did not have the customary rain shutters to protect them. The slugs were even swarming around the legs of the table.

"Where do they come from in such numbers?"

"Every typhoon season we have a lot of rain and that huge area where the training ground was gets completely flooded. No way for the water to drain off. The floors are all rotting."

"Is it like this in all the houses?"

"Yes. They were all built at the same time. It's a miracle we've managed to stand it here for seven years. We just force ourselves to stay."

Because Teiko had once lived with a relative in Tokyo for six or seven years, she spoke Tokyo dialect with a Hiroshima accent.

"The roof is made of pressed paper tiles. We used to say we'd be lucky if it lasted three years."

"There weren't any slugs when I was here last time, were there? When did they start showing up?"

"About two years ago. They began by creeping around the kitchen sink and shelves, but last year it got like this. From the middle of the rainy season last year, they started slithering out one after another even in the other tatami room and climbing up the mosquito net. Mother got up any number of times in the middle of the night and threw them into the salt water can as fast as she could catch them with the chopsticks. It made me feel so sick I couldn't sleep right until fall came."

In the six-mat room, my mother and Teiko's two daughters were asleep. My mother was seventy-four. Teiko's older daughter was seven. The younger daughter had been born after the A-bomb, proof that Teiko's reproductive organs had not been impaired by the bomb. This gave our family some measure of relief. My mother, Tsuki, and Teiko's children were sleeping soundly with their heads together. I didn't feel hungry because of the slimy slugs creeping around under the table.

"I'm sorry I come back so late every night," I said to Teiko. "Shall we go to bed now?" Teiko was actually a half-sister, my mother's child by a different marriage.

"All right," Teiko said, but she did not leave the table.

"I want to talk to you when we have some free time."

"Me, too. I want to have a nice, long talk with you sometime. You always look so busy that I can't talk to you even those few times when you come back from Tokyo."

"Well, shall we talk tonight? But maybe you're sleepy?"

A slight smile crossed Teiko's face. When she was young, people considered her pretty, but now she looked worn out. Whenever she smiled, the scars around her lips became distorted and swollen. I had something I wanted to ask her when the chance came. I sat up straight and drank a sip of my tea, which by this time had gotten cold.

"What are you going to do from now on?" I asked, having no choice but to speak in vague terms, "Mother asked me to ask you about this too. When Soichi died, Yu took the trouble to come from Fukuoka, remember? And when Yu suggested that you marry again, you got all upset and wouldn't talk to him, didn't you?"

"My husband had just died! Nobody should have said such a thing to me at that time!"

"Of course, you're right. But maybe he was half joking, the way men do. Mother thinks she understands how you felt then, so she can't bring herself to talk to you about it. But you know, it's been three years."

"The time's gone by so fast!"

"How do you feel now? You know, women who've lost their husbands often say they'd rather remain single for the sake of the children. Do you feel that way too?"

Teiko is the kind who would say she did. And if she said she wanted to stay the way she was because of the children, we would all be in an awkward position.

"The way I feel . . . ," Teiko began weakly. "I don't think I could go on alone for the rest of my life, what with two children to raise."

"I know how you must feel. I think you should marry again."

"I guess I have no choice. I admire other women who go on alone, but I can't do it."

All of a sudden, tears came to my eyes. Teiko's confession brought on unexpected thoughts, because even though I was moved by her honest reply, the idea that someone like Teiko, a widow with two children, might be able to find happiness in a second marriage seemed to be, after all, only a dream. We speak of the hardships of a woman's lot, but this was the first time I had seen them spelled out in concrete terms in the life of one of my own flesh and blood.

"You know, those dark red stone walls you go to look at so often," said Teiko. "The ones where the Tamiki Hara monument is. I used to walk through there with Konomi on my way to work at the women's hall at the exposition."

Konomi was Teiko's second daughter. She was born shortly before Soichi died. Soichi had asked me to pick out a name for her so I sent the name I had chosen from Tokyo.

"You took Konomi with you to work? Didn't Mother take care of her?"

"At first she did. But then Kumi's eye infection began spreading to everyone else and for a while Mother almost lost her sight altogether. She went groping around the house and bumping into everything. It was too dangerous for Konomi to be here with them. Besides, Mother was in a bad mood, so I left Kumi with her and took the little one with me to work every day."

I was listening to her and nodding my head.

"I stood at the sales counter all day. It was a cheap place. There was a big board like a door laid on its side and I hung things like shoulder bags, cheap shoes, stationery goods and airplane models on it. I stood there all day. I hated selling models of war planes. Anyway, the customers were all busy complaining about the admission to the exposition being so expensive, so I couldn't sell very much."

"Did Konomi play all by herself?"

"She was just beyond the toddling stage, so she fell asleep right away. Of course, there was no real place for a child to sleep. I had to let her sleep right on the ground behind me."

Teiko paused in her narrative and then went on.

"It was a springtime exposition and very dusty, and a lot of country people came even though there wasn't much to see. When I was ready to leave and would go to pick up Konomi, she would be completely white with dust. A woman at one of the other counters felt sorry for us and the next day she lent me a reed mat for Konomi to sleep on."

I could picture the child sleeping innocently on the reed mat on the ground.

"After a little while, my eyes got infected too and I quit working before the exposition closed. I was all right but I felt terrible about the children, worse than I've ever felt before. And I was bitter about the death of my husband."

Soichi didn't die in the war. He wasn't even in Hiroshima when the bomb was dropped. He was in Kyushu, after having been drafted for the third time. The troops scheduled to go to Korea were massed at the tip of Kyushu, sitting around idle; they had no arms and there were no ships to take them across. Soichi was suffering from hemorrhoids. They had gotten worse after his second period of military service. He came back from a hospital in Kyushu a month after the war ended. His home was on Nomi Island in the Inland Sea and Teiko, her daughters and Mother and I had been waiting for him there. Then one day Soichi, wearing a dirty white robe and field cap, came strolling down the island path. Mother and I watched him come toward the house. He wasn't carrying anything in his hands.

"Other men brought back as many things as they could carry in their hands or on their backs. But Soichi didn't bring back anything at all—not even a can of food or a blanket!" Mother grumbled later when she came to see me in Tokyo.

"It was okay like that," I told her, but the dissatisfied look in her face did not disappear.

Then in October of 1949, Soichi suddenly coughed up blood and ran a continuous high fever. He died almost immediately. At that time, Mother was staying with me in Tokyo. Both Mother and I were sick and, though we several times bought train tickets, we were not well enough to leave for Hiroshima. Mother finally left Tokyo on the twentieth day after his death. I had seen her aging face change drastically as a result of the sorrow she felt for her daughter. In the space of twenty days the brightness went out of her face and she grew gaunt and faded.

Strictly speaking, Soichi was not a war casualty. However, deep inside her, Mother seemed to regard Soichi Ogura as one of those killed in action. I didn't mention this to Teiko and don't intend to until she becomes aware of it herself.

"Anyway, for the rest of my life I won't forget those burned stone walls where Mr. Hara's monument stands and how Konomi and I went back and forth through there all covered with dust. I agree with you when you say the place is 'carved with the seal of history.'"

"Those aren't my words," I blurted out. "I don't say such eloquent things. That's what Mr. A from Tokyo said."

"Aside from 'the seal of history', Mr. A said that every citizen of Hiroshima from every walk of life will go on passing back and forth between those walls forever. I liked that."

Teiko and I left the three-mat room.

"Oh, look at those slugs! What are things coming to!"

3

I was riding on a streetcar running southeast through the city bound for Ujina. With me was Makoto Kikawa, who had become famous as the first officially recognized victim of the A-bomb. Every day since I had come back to Hiroshima for the first time in three years, I had met with various people and listened to their stories about the aftermath of the bomb. With eyes full of tears, I used to go with somebody like Mr. Kikawa to call on other people. Mr. Kikawa's eyes always had a dark expression of cynicism, the kind possessed by people who have known great disappointment. They were deeply tinged with enmity.

At certain moments he would show a glimpse of the willful and conceited attitude common among famous people who have been spoiled by others. And yet, he understood all too well that people had made a show of him during his long hospitalization and had almost gotten pleasure out of examining his scarred body. I had seen his keloid-covered body only in a photograph. Of course, I couldn't ask him to let me see his body. In fact I would be afraid to look at it. But today we were going to Jiai, the city hospital, and it occurred to me that, if he took off his clothes in front of the doctor, I might be able to look at his radiation-torn body with a certain degree of detachment.

He kept one hand in his pocket. It was burned and deformed like a crab's claw.

"If we have time today, would you like to see Miss Mitsuko Takada?" he asked.

"Yes, I would. She lives near the hospital, doesn't she?"

"Right behind it."

"Is it all right to visit her without letting her know we're coming? I wonder what she does for a living."

"She worked shucking oysters during the winter. I hear she's running a little store now."

Kikawa knew a lot about people like Miss Takada who barely managed to survive in Hiroshima and who tried to live away from the public eye, as though they had done something bad. With some purpose in mind, he was making a list of the disabled, collecting their signatures.

"Miss Takada has the worst face I know of," he said in a matter-of-fact and emotionless tone. After all, for seven years since the end of the war he had seen A-bomb victims day after day and mingled with those who were in much worse condition than himself.

"I think Dr. Yamazaki will be surprised. I told him I'd bring you sometime, but he doesn't know it's today. He's been wanting to see you."

"Is that so?"

When I came to Hiroshima in 1945, shortly before the end of the war, I had an operation at Jiai Hospital. Dr. Yamazaki was working under the hospital director who operated on me. There was also a young doctor who appears under his real name in John Hersey's book *Hiroshima*. Kikawa stayed in the hospital for six years after the war. He was there free of charge but he often quarreled with the doctors. He tried to organize the patients who had been wounded in the war into protesting the class discrimination reflected in the treatment given in this and other hospitals at the time. Once he made plans to escape from the hospital and go live under a bridge. But he had been operated on more than thirty times and he couldn't move around as he liked.

Kikawa had an ulterior motive in mind when he decided to go with me to Jiai Hospital. He felt bad about going there alone but he wanted to get a checkup. So it was convenient for him to visit the hospital with me because, in the past, I had gotten along quite well with all the doctors there. I, too, had another purpose in mind. One of my cousins, Taeko, had spent three and a half years in Jiai Hospital. She was a repatriate from Sariweon, Korea. I had never met her. Because both of her kidneys were tubercular, I thought that if I missed this chance, I would never be able to see my cousin's face.

The streetcar was moving through the central district of the city. We passed the bank whose stone steps had a human shadow burned into them. It was two hundred meters from ground zero. Near the bank was a new shopping street. From the window of the slowly moving streetcar, I looked at the faces of the strange men standing here and there on the streets. Their seemingly polished faces sported well-groomed beards. They were neatly dressed in bright colored clothes with shoes meticulously shined. These unknown men were a strange breed of Japanese. I had seen them, dressed in smart clothes, their bodies free of wounds, all over Hiroshima. And here and there, among the otherwise drab-looking passengers in the streetcar, were women full of vitality and without a scar, looking as though they must be these men's companions.

They wore the latest fashions and scattered through their wavy hair were dyed whirls of flaming red. I might have supposed that their hair had been burned by too much hair dryer, but in fact I had seen the same hair style many times before. From time to time, on the trains and streets, I had seen women with part of their hair in flames.

Makoto Kikawa and I got off the streetcar in front of Jiai Hospital.

4

Kikawa took off his coat in the examining room for Dr. Yamazaki, head of the surgical department. He untied his crimson tie and then removed his shirt.

Item by item he took off his clothes, seeming very much accustomed to what he was doing. Like a machine, he was doing it automatically. Because his hands were deformed, they looked like monkey paws performing the actions. Yet he was quick, without hesitation. I couldn't look at his face, but my heart was gripped by a stifling indignation.

Probably neither the doctor nor Kikawa himself noticed how skilled his hands were, hands that for six years had learned to take off his clothes item by item so as to exhibit the body in front of countless viewers, Japanese and foreigners alike. I looked at Kikawa's stomach and back. Tears didn't come to my eyes. I was beyond tears. Part of the skin on his stomach had been grafted to his back. The scars left on his stomach had all turned to keloid. There was little skin left that could be used for grafting. I wished he would hurry up and put his clothes on again. I didn't want to look at his stomach and back any more. My purpose was not to look at the survivors in Hiroshima.

"Should I operate a couple more times?" Dr. Yamazaki asked Kikawa, who had just finished dressing.

"It's not necessary," said Kikawa with a laugh, waving his hand in a gesture of refusal. "I've had enough unless I get skin cancer."

Dr. Yamazaki avoided talking about skin cancer. He turned to me and said, "The other day a reporter came to see me from XX news agency." He mentioned the name of an American newspaper which had dispatched a correspondent.

"He wanted to ask me if I thought the Americans should use an A-bomb in the Korean War."

Dr. Yamazaki, Kikawa and I were sitting in casually arranged chairs in the small room that had been rebuilt after the bomb damage.

"I told him absolutely not! Dr. X was with me and he agreed it would be absolutely wrong. He got quite excited about it."

X was the young doctor that John Hersey had written about in *Hiroshima*.

"He asked me how I felt now about the Americans dropping the bomb on Hiroshima. I said maybe the bombing of Hiroshima couldn't have been helped if it was necessary to end the war. But since they must have been able to see the terrible damage from the air, they were absolutely wrong to drop the second bomb on Nagasaki. Then Dr. X got very angry again and said that both bombs were wrong, that dropping the first one on Hiroshima was absolutely wrong, too."

"Right! That's exactly right!" I blurted out. "It would have been wrong even to use it to end the war, but that wasn't why they used it. They used it in a hurry because they were afraid of losing their military balance of power with the Soviet Union. It was the first step in their present world policy."

"Do you know how many people were killed in Hiroshima?"

"How many?"

"Five hundred thousand."

I had seen the same figure somewhere else. It was in the newspaper in Hiroshima. I was not surprised that the figures from the newspaper and the hospital matched.

The doctor spread a piece of paper on the desk. He got a pencil and started drawing something. He drew a castle in the background of the picture. Beside the castle he wrote "divisional headquarters." I thought next he would sketch those stone walls attached to the castle and start writing Tamiki Hara's poetry there, but I was wrong. Instead, he drew several rectangles and put letters in each one.

"This is the army hospital, this is the second annex building, and this the first annex. Next to it is the artillery, and here are the first and second west units. And here is the transport corps. There must have been a couple of temporary hospitals, too."

The doctor, himself a victim of the A-bomb, announced in the candid manner of a surgeon, "Almost all the soldiers in this building that morning were killed instantly."

For a while I stared at the rectangle that the doctor had drawn on the white paper for the first west unit. One of my brothers-in-law had died there. None of his bones were recovered. As I remembered our childhood together, his shiny white teeth flashed through my mind.

"There were seven hundred thousand people in Hiroshima that day."

"That many? I thought there were only four hundred thousand and two-thirds of them were killed."

"The army personnel weren't included in the count. It was casually announced that such and such units were stationed in such and such places, and there were a lot of people going in and out at that time. At Mutual Benefit Hospital alone, there were five thousand people, and most of them were killed. The figure, five thousand reminds me that the Germans used a poison gas on the Ypres front for the first time during World War I. Five thousand soldiers were killed in three days as a result of the chlorine gas. Because it was such a cruel weapon, it became an international issue and then someone put forward a proposal to ban the use of poison gas."

Dr. Yamazaki spoke in a voice heavy with emotion. Then he added, "America didn't ratify the ban on poison gas at that time."

Kikawa had been resting his back against the window frame as he listened to Dr. Yamazaki. In a low, indifferent-sounding voice, he said, "The office at ground zero is now registering the names of A-bomb victims and putting together statistics. I hear they are surprised at the number of people who were killed."

The general assumption that two hundred thousand perished instantly was no exaggeration. However, that figure had for the sake of convenience been too quickly accepted as definitive. The figure was a miscalculation because all it meant was that some two hundred thousand people had died instantly. The citizens who failed to die that first day had died one after another in the days that followed. For months and years, people died in great numbers, until there were almost as many delayed deaths as there had been instantaneous deaths.

It had started raining. We decided to visit Mitsuko Takada at once.

"I'm not using my car, so why don't you take it?" the surgeon said. "Mr. Kikawa, you could go with her to Motomachi."

I decided to borrow Dr. Yamazaki's small car because of the rain. The thought of visiting my cousin came to mind for a moment, but there was no time to mention it. Kikawa and I drove through the rain in the small car.

At the foot of a bridge misty with rain, a makeshift wooden building, painted pale blue, came into view.

"There it is!"

Even before Kikawa pointed it out, I had guessed that it must be Mitsuko's house. It was a little bread and milk store, which had the friendly, inviting look peculiar to this town. From the car, I could see bread, candy, soft drinks and milk in a showcase in the middle of the dirt floor. Inside was a man in his fifties, his hair getting thin. I caught a glimpse of the back of a girl in a shabby, black dress, but she disappeared through a door in the rear of the store.

"She's changing her clothes," the elderly man said to me and smiled good-naturedly after Kikawa had spoken to him. Seating myself on a board at the foot of the entrance and holding the gift I had brought in my lap, I waited for the girl. Then she appeared and my breath stopped. This small girl must have been the one I saw in the black dress going inside.

It was not a girl but a monstrosity. Her deformed face and hands stood out even more grotesquely because she had put on her best clothes, a pure white blouse and a skirt with a flower pattern in crisp white. It seemed as though she was deliberately thrusting herself at me. Her face was expressionless and she didn't even greet me. I broke down weeping, slumped on the wooden board, shuddering but unable to stop my tears. I wished I could stand up, reach out to the monstrous body of the young woman and embrace it. However, Japanese people, and I especially, are not accustomed to expressing their emotions in that way.

I still couldn't stop weeping, sobbing loudly, my face pressed to the wooden board. The brazen instincts of the writer deserted me and I was no more than a plain, defenseless human being. The girl, standing motionless in the middle of the dirt floor, was observing me. Then she came nearer.

"It's all right. I've learned to accept it," Mitsuko said, and lifted me up in her arms. I was going to say, "Don't accept it!" but the words wouldn't come out. Still sobbing, I placed the gift in Mitsuko's hands. Her fingers were burned exactly the same as Kikawa's and they bent inward. The skin was shriveled and dark brown.

"I'm sorry," I said, continuing to cry. "I'm not a reporter, but because I'm a novelist I came here to ask you a few questions. I have a pad and pencil in my handbag. But I can't ask you anything today . . . ."

Mitsuko, who was young enough to be my daughter, said gently, "Would you like some milk?" She poured milk from a bottle into a glass and brought it to me with a straw. Kikawa, sitting in a chair, was drinking a bottle of soda pop. I was still feeling deeply depressed, and I thought I would become ill if I lived through many more tear-filled days like this one.

"Why don't you come inside and sit down and relax," Mitsuko said, seeming to open up to me, probably because I was crying so hard and because I had told her that I wouldn't ask her any questions. Pushing open a door, she led Kikawa and me into a room overlooking the river. The floor was tilted, the ceiling seemed about to fall in, and the walls were crumbling.

"Half of this house almost fell into the river that day. Later we pulled it back up and repaired it so we could at least sleep here," her father, the elderly man we had seen earlier, explained as he sat down beside me.

The mouth of an inlet near Ujina Bay was barely visible in the rain. Then he started talking about things I wanted to know.

"My daughter's face got like this when she was fourteen. I want her to have some operations or something as soon as possible, but she's only nineteen now. She's still a child and the doctor said it wouldn't be any good for her to have operations now while she's still growing. That's why we've put it off."

"Please give her the chance to have an operation as soon as possible, so she can get better, even a little . . . ."

"We raise oysters in Ujina Bay and every year the typhoons practically wipe them out. Oyster farming's our business, but if the beds are destroyed we have no way to get through the following year. So there's not enough money, even though we want her to have operations."

I wanted to get the conversation off such grim topics. Turning to Mitsuko, I asked, "About the oyster beds—can anyone farm oysters?"

Mitsuko who had not shed a tear in my presence, replied in

an ordinary tone of voice, with no trace of gloom.

"Oyster beds are like farm land—you buy so many lots. So you can't just go on and on buying lots."

Kikawa smiled. "So when they're wiped out, it's like losing a year's worth of crops. That's pretty bad!"

I leaned over the railing of the window for a while and gazed at the line where the sea and the river meet, my favorite kind of scenery. Then I drew a rough map showing how to get to Teiko's house and handed it to Mitsuko.

"I'll come again but please stop by when you feel like it."

"I will. I'll bring some fish from my father's catch," Mitsuko replied quickly.

The rain was coming down harder. Shortly after we had gotten into the car and started off, Kikawa asked thoughtfully, "What do you think about this idea? I'm planning to take the signatures of the A-bomb sufferers to General MacArthur's Headquarters in Tokyo. Maybe they would contribute some money for rehabilitation. I want to go right away if possible."

"Don't do it!" I said, "The more you look to them for help, the more you'll be disappointed. If they had had any thought about the sufferings of A-bomb victims, they wouldn't have dropped such a thing in the first place!"

"You don't think it would work?"

I had in mind an article I'd read in a newspaper. It was about a women's group that organized a protest against the raising of electricity rates. They went to see the director of resources at General Headquarters and asked him to support the movement, but all he did was shout at them, "It's only been forty years since Japan first began using electricity. Electricity is a luxury for you! If you don't like the rate hike, then get some candles!" I didn't know whether that's actually what happened, but I told Kikawa the story anyway because it seemed symbolic to me.

"Is that so?" he said, "But I'll go at least once. Regardless of what happens, I intend to."

"I sometimes think I should take ten girls like Mitsuko Takada and stand them in line so those people could see their faces. But I don't know how they'd react."

The heavy rain continued to beat down on the small car.

5

Since I had been staying up late almost every night, I was still in bed a little before noon. Someone seemed to have come. I thought I heard the clear voice of a young woman calling from the dirt floored area, one step in from outside, that served as the entrance hall to Teiko's shack, and then I thought I heard my mother's voice. And yet after that the house was silent.

Teiko was not at home because of her work and Kumi was at school. I started dozing off again when I heard my mother sobbing. It sounded as though her chest were choked with pain. Her weeping continued for some time. Then she came and knelt down beside where I was sleeping.

"Miss Takada, the one you told me about, is here."

"All right."

I got up quickly and took off my night clothes. With my mother's help I folded up the bedding.

"You've told me about her, but what an awful face she has! So sad I couldn't help crying . . . ." She continued to weep as she put the bedding away. Mitsuko came in. She was wearing the same white skirt with the flower pattern that I had seen last time, along with a white jacket. Her outfit was very cheery. But her walk lacked the carefree ease common to young women her age. The radiation had burned and shriveled even her toes, so that Mitsuko walked like a cripple, with a tottering gait.

"I've brought you something you might like."

As soon as she came into the six-mat room and sat down, she united the knot of the bundle she was carrying. With her twisted brown fingers, she pulled open the purple wrapping cloth.

"What is it?"

I unwrapped the newspaper from around the bundle, not expecting to find anything of great value. When I finally got it all open I discovered it was full of river crabs.

"My father and I caught them in the river and boiled them. Please eat them if you'd like."

"Thank you."

I remembered that my aunt had died suddenly at the age of twenty-nine after eating river crabs, but I could hardly tell Mitsuko that. Mitsuko said she was going to a Shochiku musical show today because she had gotten a ticket through the store-keepers' association she belonged to. The troupe was performing at the new culture center that had been built on a burned-out field in the old military ground.

"Miss Saeko Ozuki is performing with the troupe. The show starts at one o'clock, so I wanted to come to see you before that."

I felt odd when I thought of this girl's face among the audience watching Saeko Ozuki dance with the Shochiku troupe.

"Then why don't you have lunch here?"

"Thank you but I brought a box lunch. Still, maybe I won't go to the center. I guess I won't."

"Why not?"

"I don't feel like going anymore."

"You don't want to be stared at, is that it?"

I pressed ahead with more questions. I felt that I was trying to win the heart of a little girl. The calculations of the writer consciously rose in my mind. By making friends with this young girl, I'll be able to understand what's in the bottom of her heart. But, as though to transcend such calculations, my mind adopted a cool approach.

"I don't mind them looking at my face. I go alone to movie theaters without any hesitation and I walk proudly down the center of the main street," she said. It was a sad statement.

"At the spring festival held by the storekeepers' association this year, I got up on stage and danced. I knew it made the other people feel uneasy, but still I went up on the stage with this face . . . ."

She paused for a moment.

"I was dancing around, laughing and crying, and I thought I must look like a monkey or an ogre or something. Then the audience started crying out loud."

My eyes were full of tears. And yet Mitsuko's were dry. She didn't shed a single tear. She seemed to be trying to take revenge on somebody. Mitsuko talked in bursts, with short pauses in between.

"For a while I was going to church. I'd heard they would save people. But not people like me. Because we don't have any real intention of looking to them for help."

"So you quit going? Why?"

"A foreign lady was coming to the church and she always stared at my hands with a sorrowful expression on her face. And then she went to a lot of trouble and made a pair of gloves out of red yarn specially designed to fit my hands. After that, I quit going to church once and for all."

Two-year-old Konomi came in with a candy bowl full of rice crackers and put it down between Mitsuko and me. Konomi sat down and stared at Mitsuko's face without blinking.

"I guess there must be different kinds of foreign ladies. Another lady took a couple of pictures of me and then she turned aside and started looking for something in her handbag. She pulled out fifty or sixty yen and pressed it on me. I didn't want to take the money, but then her interpreter said I should because refusing it would be even ruder than accepting."

"Maybe they don't know anything about Japanese money."

"Yes, they do. Some people slip about twenty yen or more into my hand. They think I'm some kind of exhibition from the zoo. It's written on their faces."

As I grew accustomed to looking at her face, I realized that there was a certain expression in her eyes, where the skin around them was burned and stretched vertically. Her eyes were calm and seemed to be smiling gently.

"My eye is shining, isn't it?"

"Shining?"

"After that day, this eye shines more than the other. I can feel it myself."

Then, after being silent for a while, she said, "I want to be a gentle person."

"What would you like to do in the future?"

"I want to grow up fast and help people who're having a hard time. I wish I could be thirty years old right now. I keep thinking about it."

Mother fixed lunch for two. Konomi tried to lift up the table with a childish grunt. Mother and Konomi together brought in the food. Mitsuko spilled rice when she ate. Her lips were askew and the lower lip, having lost its natural shape, drooped in an unsightly fashion. Any kind of food was bound to drop out of her mouth. She had no choice but to push it down her throat as she ate. After eating only a little, she put her chopsticks down on the table.

"Don't you have to go to see Saeko Ozuki?"

"I don't feel like going today," she said. "If you don't mind, I'd rather spend some more time with you."

I took her for a walk. I had an impulse to take this monster-like Mitsuko and parade around town with her. And yet I found myself walking in the direction of the deserted places.

"Shall we go to the old castle site?"

"All right."

Between the rows of makeshift huts such as the one Teiko

lived in, summer flowers were blooming here and there along the narrow paths. Every shack had flowers and vegetables growing in its fenced-in yard. They seemed to be a sign that people don't want to die but just want to go on living.

The water in the moat was stagnant and green, with duck-weed floating on the surface. We came to the stone wall. The stones looked as though they were burning. They were on fire with bright and rusty reds, light greens and faint yellows burning in a melancholy fashion, like the printed cotton of olden times.

"Right here they're going to put up a monument to a poet who committed suicide."

"I read about him in the paper. Why did he commit suicide?"

"Nobody really understands about suicide. Some people say Tamiki Hara had suicidal tendencies anyway, even if he hadn't been terrified by memories of the bomb. Maybe they're right. But I can't help but think that Mr. Hara's suicide had something to do with the A-bomb," I added, as though talking to myself. "As long as 'Summer Flower', 'Requiem' and 'The Land of Heart's Desire' exist," I said, naming some of Tamiki Hara's works, "I have to think so."

"When the monument is erected," I said, "please come here sometime to see it. I can't come here that often from Tokyo."

"I'll certainly pay a visit on your behalf every August 6."

"The anniversary of his death is March 13th. Will you remember that for me?"

Mitsuko and I walked across the former training ground toward the downtown area. We came to the streetcar stop at Aioi Bridge. Without any real purpose in mind, we got on a streetcar.

I got back to Teiko's house after dark. The smell of grass filled the space between the rows of huts. I used the old horse trough as a landmark in finding my way to Teiko's shack. A firefly flickered in the grass.

The fireflies were not big enough to fly yet. I squatted down. Here and there the slender fireflies were flashing their lights in the clumps of grass. I picked one up.

"Mr. Soldier!" I said. "You must be the ghost of a dead soldier. Can't you break away? Shortly after you people died, the war ended. You're not soldiers anymore, so fly! Fly up high!"

I tried tossing the firefly high up into the air. It floated down lightly. Down in the grass, all the fireflies were glowing.

It seemed to me that it was not only the fireflies that were the ghosts of the dead soldiers. I came to feel the same about the slugs that slithered around the shack from evening till late at night. Even after Mother, Teiko and the children had fallen asleep, I was still awake. The three-mat room was like a house for slugs. I said to them, "You must have been soldiers. You come here every night because you have something you want to say. Can't you ever rest in peace?"

That is a frank expression of the way I felt.

translated by Kōichi Nakagawa

Ineko Sata

The Colorless Paintings

I'M standing in a gallery of an art museum, with my eyes on two oil paintings, silent. Y is beside me, also silently looking at them. Y is taller than I am. She's holding her handbag clutched under her left arm, with her right hand pressed against her cheek. The way she presses her cheek suggests that by doing so she is just barely able to hold back some inward turmoil. There is a little distance between us and the paintings, and we are staring at them without a word.

On the day in question, we got off the train at Uguisudani and walked along beside the row of stone lanterns that have for years lined the road to the Tokyo National Museum grounds. The sky was somewhat cloudy, an autumn day without sunshine. In front of the museum there were the usual junior high school students drawn up in lines and waiting to go in, and here and there were stands selling sweets and sandwiches. A man with a box slung from his neck was peddling ice cream. Inside the gate, visitors with their backs to us crossed the wide plaza in front of the museum, strolling leisurely under the cloudy sky. There was no crowding or confusion, and even the ice cream vendor's cries were not particularly loud. We were in a little area of calm preserved for the citizens of Tokyo, and beyond it, the tall brown museum building presented its entrance, flanked by stone columns and approached by a flight of broad stone steps. Y, Y's brother-in-law, and I hurried toward the entrance, as though going to meet someone, and ascended the flight of steps.

It was the first day of an exhibition held by a prestigious fine arts group, today open only to those with invitations. We entered the first room, then the second, and of course all the rooms were alive with color. In one room, hung entirely with abstract paintings, there was a flood of black and primary colors such as yellow and red. The powerful colors seemed to dance up out of the paintings, like bursts of pure energy. As I walked along, I peered at the paintings beyond the onlookers, searching above all for the works of one particular painter. Searching through the works on exhibition, I felt I must find them as quickly as possible. Perhaps the two people with me already knew where his pictures were. Without even thinking whether that might be the case, I searched for the paintings in room after room.

I was looking for K's pictures. I had seen K's work once several years ago at this place. The fact that I had seen K's work only once, while he had been showing it annually for over a dozen years, merely proved how lazy I was, considering my friendly relations with him. K had not come up to Tokyo each year when his work was shown. Now I realized that perhaps he had not been able to afford the trip. That was the reason why, several years ago when I came here to look at his work, I made a point of writing to K to tell him my impressions, since he could not attend the exhibition himself.

The two paintings shown here at that time were elegant landscapes keyed in soft pink. They expressed K's gentle nature, as well as his fastidiousness. There was something restrained in their graceful beauty, something neat and trim. They reflected

K's personality and features exactly.

K's high-bridged nose and bushy eyebrows conveyed an impression of masculinity, but he was suffering from tuberculosis, which made his eyes bright and luminous, with a tinge of peevishness in them. I tried to imagine him making posters for the Communist Party—K was associated with the party at that time—but I couldn't quite picture what kind of posters they would be. K's paintings at that time were done in beautiful colors.

I have come here today to see a posthumous showing of K's works. A few days ago K's younger brother N came up from Nagasaki, bringing K's last paintings. My friend Y has come up with him because she wants to see them in the setting where they will be exhibited. Y is older than N and is his sister-in-law, but she is not K's wife. Y is not married. She is N's sister-in-law because her younger sister married N. And so to K she was a sister-in-law by marriage. But even before she became related to him by marriage she was a very close friend of K's and a supporter of his work. Y is a Chinese businesswoman who lives in Nagasaki, and K must have given her considerable moral support as well. I know a little about their friendship. Less than two months have passed since K's death, and Y and N are very much emotionally involved in this posthumous exhibition of his works.

After passing through several roomfuls of profuse colors, we are standing now in front of K's paintings. "Ah!" I say, but after that I can't say anything more. I stand in silence. Y of course knows these paintings very well. Yet she presses her hand against her cheek as if she could hardly contain her feelings.

Only to us are the paintings powerful and moving. They are colorless, done entirely in shades of white tinged with gray. Both are landscapes. One, abstract in style, has a foreground with two trees in it, looking as if they were a sheet of stretched cloth. The other depicts three thin, withered trees painted in slight gradations of white and gray. They remind me of the dead trees standing in the swamps in Kamikōchi.

Framed in thin white pieces of wood, the pictures, surrounded by a world of bright colors, seem like softly moaning heretics. Between the paintings, a little higher up on the wall, is a small photograph of the artist in a black frame with a black ribbon tied on it. This might make the impression of the paintings stick with people. Visitors will say to themselves, "Ah, the paintings of a dead man! I see." The pictures even remind us of burnt bones.

The photograph hanging a little above the pictures shows the handsome, striking face of K as he was when he was alive. He is wearing a beret. People will glance at it and know only that a painter has died. Of course, they will think, people get sick and die, and a painter's life in particular is full of troubles. K's face, the black ribbon, these colorless pictures, may tell them that and nothing more.

We don't know what to say, facing these paintings, except to stare at them silently. I don't know how he actually painted these thin, withered trees with their branches sticking out, all done in gradations of pale white. But here the paintings are, and that's what they depict. The days when K painted these existed as surely as the paintings exist now. Until the paintings were painted, the people around him had not known about his fatal disease. K himself, though irritated by extreme fatigue, would not have known why he got so tired. If so, then why did K's paintings have to turn out to be dead trees done in pale white, nothing but pale white?

N, K's brother, leans over to me and, sounding as though

he's on the verge of tears, whispers, "See! There's no color at all!"

These few words are no doubt meant to convey a great deal of meaning.

I have one oil painting by K in my home. It's a scene of the hilly part of Nagasaki, with bright sky and a pink Western-style house set among brilliant green trees. The colors are clear and shimmering. The hills are the area in Nagasaki where foreigners used to live, and the whole picture, in its quiet dignity, suggests a scene in some foreign country. In this picture, the sharply defined colors play a kind of beautiful music.

K has three children. He once said to me, "I'm even fonder of my children than most parents."

And yet these posthumous paintings of his completely deny all color. K, while painting them, repeatedly rejected color. To me, and needless to say to Y and N too, the paintings are powerful precisely because they are colorless, because we see them as an honest expression of the violent drama that took place inside him, purity withdrawing into itself, which was characteristic of K. K was never capable of trickery. The only course open to him was to go on eliminating colors and leave it at that.

It was early this summer when Y wrote me about her own physical weakening. She mentioned it casually while thanking me for a small gift:

Around that time I began to feel sick and discovered things like spots on my body, so I went to the A-bomb Hospital and got a thorough examination. They gave me a radiation victim's certificate for having been within the radiation area on that day. I didn't think I could be suffering from the effects of the bomb, but I went to the hospital every day for examinations anyway. I have no confidence in my health these days, and as a result, when anything like this happens I tend to worry and be overanxious about my physical condition. But recently the results of the examinations finally came in, and it turns out that the spots on my skin are nothing malignant. They are apparently due to some kind of deficiency caused by gastroptosis.

To me, even this letter was startling. Whenever I returned to Nagasaki, my home town, I used to see K and Y, and often stayed at their homes, and yet I was insensitive enough to assume that they had no connection with the atomic bomb. It seems I took it for granted that they had somehow been outside of the radiation area when the bomb was dropped on Nagasaki. I never realized, until it came out in a casual letter, that all this time Y had been living with that kind of anxiety. Y mentioned it lightly, and lightly, it seemed, she had denied her anxiety. Up to now, Y's letters had always been light and restrained in tone like this. But this letter, after lightly mentioning the results of her examinations, was somehow different in tone. Yet at the time I did not think that the tone had any deep connection with the bomb.

Y wrote that in Nagasaki, as in other areas of Japan, demonstrations were going on every day and said she could see a lot of people passing by her house. And then she said, "I feel impatient because, being a foreigner in Japan, I can't join them, and so I have no way to show my feelings by expressing them in some concrete form." Unlike her earlier letters, the tone in this passage was passionate. At that time, the protests against the revision of the U.S.-Japan Security Pact were at their height. I felt that, as a foreigner living in Japan, she was deeply agitated about the situation, and I perused her words carefully. The letter continued:

Today again my friends went to the prefectural meeting. I envy them and am suddenly irritated.

Looking back, I feel that as foreigners we are much freer now, without the kind of restrictions that were placed on us in the past.

We are free now from the feelings of humiliation that were un-consciously instilled in us from the time we were children. As long as we keep up an interest in the things around us, we can maintain a balanced outlook on life. In the past, all the Chinese in Japan had to do, to put it somewhat bluntly, was to close their eyes to what went on around them and concentrate on making money and getting by. The world of Chinese business people in Japan had no windows to look out of. But I envy those who can join the demonstrations. I feel irritated with myself and my environ-ment and cut off from others. Is this because in my own way I have some kind of discontent and feeling of resistance in me?

In the letter, she revealed her inner emotions in a way she never had before. The times I had seen her when I was back in Nagasaki, she had scarcely ever spoken to me in so familiar and intense a fashion. But even the passage above, of course, is not directly related to the atomic bomb. And because she and the others normally adopted such a casual attitude, I had forgotten that they had been exposed to radiation. K was no exception in this respect.

At the beginning of August, about two months after I re-ceived this letter from Y, she wrote me again, this time notify-ing me that K had gone into the hospital. The letter, describing the progress of K's ailment since his hospitalization in July, was hurriedly written and rather incoherent in places, conveying to me how serious K's condition was and how distressed Y felt about it. Before I had had time to write to her, a telegram arrived informing me of K's death. The cause of death, to put it briefly, was cancer of the liver.

It was a while later that Y wrote me the details on the devel-opment of K's sickness up to the time of his death. It had become impossible for him to urinate, she said, and they could not prevent abdominal dropsy from developing, no matter how they tried. He had grown as skinny as an old man.

"I want a glass of water," he had said to her in a voice as feeble as the buzz of a mosquito. When she gave him a piece of ice to hold in his mouth, he crunched it up as though he were suffering from extreme thirst. After mentioning how often he had asked for a drink of water, Y described the rapid worsening of the disease and the way he died, covering over ten pages of writing paper with her wail of grief.

She said that toward the end K mentioned me once. "She'll be coming to Nagasaki next year, won't she? For the anti-nuclear rally," he said.

When they had the world meeting in Nagasaki to ban atomic and hydrogen bombs, I went down to attend, and I stayed upstairs above Y's cozy coffee shop near where I had lived in the old days. I wonder if K remembered that when he was dying. It was an unforgettable time to me.

Y's coffee shop was in a busy part of town, the buildings around it built so close that there was no space in between them. Y's place did not have a bath in the house. I knew that, but I thought I would just go to a public bath in the neighborhood.

When I arrived, however, I found K out on a platform for drying laundry that opened off the upstairs window, busily hammering nails and putting up bamboo blinds. I was told he was building a temporary bathing place for me.

"It's hot here in Nagasaki. When you come back from the meeting, it will be nicer if you can take a bath right here and wash off the sweat," he said.

K, with the versatility that goes with being a painter, screened in the place so that no one could see in from outside. After the bamboo blinds were up, he put sheets of blue vinyl over them and it became a bathing place. The tub was surrounded by blue vinyl walls, and all one had to do was bring up some hot water from downstairs and my bath was ready!

I remembered that Nagasaki people used to take baths in a tub every evening. Pierre Loti mentioned it in *Madame Chrysan-thème*, saying how surprised he was to have naked women greet him from their tubs as though it were a matter of course. I was brought up in that custom and thought nothing of taking a bath inside blue vinyl walls. There was no space at the rear of the coffee shop to put the tub, so the clothes-drying platform next to the upstairs window would be used for that purpose instead—that was all. It was considerate of K. K was not the kind who would attend the anti-nuclear meeting and get up and make a speech. But he built a bathing place on the laundry platform so I could wash myself as soon as I got back from the meeting. I knew he did it not only for my convenience but as a token of his desire to participate in some way in the meeting.

The city of Nagasaki, with mountains on three sides and only one side open to the sea, can be stifling at evening, when the breeze from the sea dies down and the fierce heat sits so heavily on the streets that all sounds are muted. Every day as soon as I got back from the day's meeting I jumped inside the blue walls on the laundry platform as fast as I could. Even though I was wearing sleeveless clothes, my skin was wet with perspiration. When the tub was filled with hot water carried up in buckets from downstairs, I sat in it and washed my back and shoulders with a washcloth. If I stretched out my arm, I could reach the upstairs window of the house in back of the coffee shop. The house was at the end of an alley where there were a lot of women, perhaps some kind of place of prostitution. It was too early for any customers to be around, but I could hear women's footsteps climbing up and down the stairs. Above my vinyl enclosure was the evening sky of Nagasaki. It spread over the rooftops, whitish, an impassive light lingering still. Sitting in the tub naked, I looked up at the sky and heard the footsteps of people coming and going and the automobile horns on the street below. But no one on the street could see me bathing alone on the roof.

Then I would get out of the tub and empty the water little by little on the roof. If I emptied it all at once, the rain pipe would clog and the water would overflow and splash into the window next door. K and the others would wait in the nearby room while I took my bath, talking together. I could sense in the atmosphere the friendliness and consideration they felt for me. And the consideration of K and the others did not stop at the makeshift bathing arrangement on the laundry platform.

"K changed the covering on the tatami mats by himself," Y said to me. "He thought our tatami were too dirty, I'm sure."

I couldn't believe her words. "He lifted up these heavy mats?"

"Oh, it's easy to change the covering," K remarked casually. "You just put on a new covering and sew it up."

"What a bothersome guest I've turned out to be!" I said.

"I can do that much for you at least, when you came all the way down here for the meeting," he said.

So the two tatami rooms opening onto each other had new covering for their mats. On the last night, when the meetings were all over, I sat up writing a piece to send to a Tokyo publisher in one of the rooms, keeping Y from getting a proper night's sleep.

I had known K for quite some time. During the war K came to Tokyo with his wife and lived there for a while. I had known him since that time. I came to know Y through K when I went back to Nagasaki on three or four occasions. She was always reserved, probably, as she said in her letter, because the Chinese living in Japan were subject to certain pressures. But during the meeting I have been talking about, for the first time I saw the lively side of her, and it made a deep impression on me. Chinese representatives attended the meeting, and that served as a source of encouragement to the meeting and the Japanese victims of the bomb. Y, who usually doesn't talk much, talked unusually freely when the subject was the Chinese representatives.

It was in the midst of such an atmosphere that Y spoke for the first time about the day when the atomic bomb was dropped. And because she had done so, K also spoke about it, he too for the first time. When describing the tragic scene, K seemed to be walking back and forth in the midst of the ruins.

"Were you like that, too?" I asked.

"Yes, I was. Every day I walked among corpses."

He had never mentioned that experience until then. Partly this was because in my insensitivity I had never tried to find out about those days. And even after I heard about how K and his friends had wandered around in the radiated area, I somehow thought of them as having been outside the radiation. Since K had been close to the Communist Party, we found a common topic of interest in talking about the party's activities. At other times I listened to K tell of the irritations he encountered in the field of fine arts. K endured severe poverty. But hearing him express disapproval of the sumptuous manner in which Tokyo artists lived, I thought him a bit fastidious.

"You've put on weight. You were better when you were thinner."

That's what K once told me. K implied that he was talking about more than just my weight. I sensed a certain displeasure in his words. I felt I understood what he meant, but, apart from that, I thought of K's fastidious narrowness and of a certain masochistic element in his suffering. K himself talked about these tendencies in his makeup the next time we met, and for that reason I came to think of his narrowness as in a way beautiful. The people around him said that K's poverty, in the face of the fact that he had a wife and children to support, was due to his unusual degree of purity.

"I know I'm like that," K would say in reply, "and yet I can't do the way other people do." He looked as if he were perplexed with himself for being so hopeless. His wife was a shy woman who relied on him entirely, and his three children were darling.

So, K was not the way he was because he lacked the will power to act differently. When he had a one-man show in Nagasaki, he sent me photographs of it, and not long ago he told me he was planning to have a one-man show in Tokyo. He seemed to be enjoying himself teaching painting to young workmen and children.

In any event, I do not think the loss of color in K's paintings derived from any loss of vitality in his will. Y's letter describing K's fatal illness also shows his longing for life. Y said she told him that when he got a little better he should go somewhere in the country to recuperate, though Y herself knew that, sad as it was, such a day would never come. And K, as if dreaming of that day, had said, "Yes, indeed. It would be nice to dip my feet in a little stream in the country." She says he told his other friends about his hopes, too. "When I get better, I'm going to the country to recuperate!"

The reason color went out of K's paintings was at least not a weakening of the will to live. I go on standing in front of K's colorless paintings and look at his photograph with the black ribbon, painfully holding back the thoughts that well up in me. I want to say something to the people viewing the pictures. I want to say something to the visitors who look at K's paintings and display a polite attitude of sorrow before his photograph and then pass on. The landscape with its dead trees painted in grayish white, backed up by the message of the black ribbon, suggests death. If they look at these paintings in the light of that suggestion, then there is something I have to say to them: No, no. K himself could not have been aware of his impending death.

The disease that killed him, after inflicting rapidly increasing pain, was cancer of the liver. The natural result of physical emaciation was expressed here in the paintings—is that the right conclusion? The inevitable relation between the artistic production and the physical power of the artist is verified by the black ribbon.

No, that's not true, I would still insist. I want to say something, because the paintings devoid of color and the photograph with the mourning band tell us that and nothing more. And yet I cannot express it clearly. I myself am afraid to probe into the matter. The name of the disease is liver cancer. But what is the name of the thing that deprived this man of all color? What could it be called? It seems that the ideas suggested by these paintings preclude anything that is commonplace. They appear to belong to another realm. They rather seem to be produced by the will to defy, but that defiance had to be painted, even though colors escaped the artist, and that's why they display an unnameable grief. But this will probably not be apparent to the visitors passing from gallery to gallery. People seem to trust to the impression they get from the black ribbon as they stand in front of the paintings that have lost all color.

Y sways and takes a step forward. It seems as though her body automatically sways and takes a step. As if her surroundings were not even within her field of vision, her eyes gleam gravely, expressing intense feeling. Y must have sensed deep in her heart what the colorless paintings are saying.

translated by Shiloh Ann Shimura

Kyōko Hayashi

The Empty Can

THE school was a four storied, U-shaped building. The five of us were standing in about the center of the yard it enclosed. It was past 1:30 in the afternoon. The sun had begun to shift toward the west, and the school building cast its shadow across the yard. The place where the five of us were standing was already in shadow. But the auditorium, which faced toward the west, was still flooded with sunlight.

"And now a word about the use of the lavatories," said Oki, facing the other four, hands on hips. "Who was it who always used to say that?" Nishida asked, pointing at Oki, trying to remember. Who was that anyway? There was definitely one teacher who was always lecturing us about the use of the lavatories. "Scrub brush!" I shouted, remembering his nickname. Hara gave the sleeve of my overcoat a tug, and warned me in the gentle way so characteristic of the Nagasaki dialect. "Careful—they'll hear you in the faculty room." But the teachers of thirty years ago couldn't be in the faculty room now. Not only the teachers of thirty years ago. There was no one left in the faculty room now.

Our alma mater was to be closed at the end of next year. The students had already moved to the new school, which had been built on a height overlooking the city of Nagasaki. The phoenix palm that was once planted by the circular driveway at the entrance had been dug up, and lay with its roots wrapped in straw matting—we had seen it when we entered the school gate a little while before. There had been a phoenix palm by the circular driveway when we were high school girls. Judging from the shape of the branches, this was probably the same tree. In thirty years' time this phoenix, which branched off into three trees near the root, had grown to a height of 7 or 8 meters. Would it, too, be transplanted to the grounds of the new school?

We were the only ones on the school grounds. The school had absorbed all sound into its concrete surface, and stood in silence like a castle wall.

We were often called together in this yard when there was a special announcement. The teacher Oki had imitated was a man science teacher. When the announcement was over, he would turn, and with a "Well now . . ." begin to address the students, bustling over to climb the platform the faculty used when we had our morning exercises. Then, in just the tone of Oki's imitation, he would start. "And now a word about the use of the lavatories." The correct way to dispose of sanitary napkins, and to flush the toilets; he would explain in great detail all the rules of proper usage. Especially during the winter, when the pipes of the toilets would freeze, the water would overflow on the outside, making a white water stain on the outside wall of the building which severely detracted from the aesthetic appearance of the school. He would point at the stain in admonition. Those were the rough days just after the war, but we were young girls after all, and we were embarrassed by such talk. That was probably why this was the first memory to come to Oki as she stood in the school yard—embarrassment must have left a deep impression. The white stain where the water had overflowed was still there, even wider than before.

First floor, second floor, following the floors up along the surface of the wall, I turned my eyes toward the sky. The patch of clear blue sky cut into the shape of a U was right above my face. The light of the sun, which gave off a warmth unusual for early winter, gleamed along the straight concrete edge. I lowered my eyes once again to the fourth floor, then the third. The windows of the building were all closed. For a deserted school building, the glass was well polished. And there was a perfect pane of glass in each window on every floor. That was what looked strange to me.

From the time the A-bomb was dropped on August 9, 1945, until I graduated two years later, there wasn't a single pane of glass in the school. In the corners of the window frames, which the blast had warped into bowlike curves, only fragments had remained here and there, pointed like shark's teeth.

Pieces of board had been nailed over the dressing rooms and toilets, where a screen of some kind was needed, but that was only in the places where the steel window frames were straight.

How had they mended each warped window frame? The window frames, divided vertically and horizontally into many sections, were perfectly straight, and panes of transparent glass were fitted into them, just as they had been then. If you looked carefully you could see that the now popular aluminum type sash had been installed in five or six of the windows on the auditorium side. The windows were divided into two parts, upper and lower, and only in those places the frames caught the western sun, gleaming silver in its light. They must have been put in to replace the windows that were damaged beyond repair, but their flashy newness stuck out next to the white water stain and the rusty iron window frames smeared with putty.

"Was the yard really this small?" said Nishida, looking around.

"I was just thinking the same thing," said Hara, glancing around the yard along with Nishida.

"Want to take a look inside?" asked Noda, who was dressed

in kimono.

"Yeah, let's go in," said Oki. "I want to get a last look at the auditorium." I, too, wanted to see the auditorium one more time before it was torn down.

We walked toward the student entrance. There was an iron lock on the entrance. We cut through the yard, and through the main entrance, dirty with the earth from the uprooted phoenix palm, we entered the school.

The instant that we stood in the entrance of the auditorium, the five of us stopped our chattering. Each one stood stock still, as if nailed to the spot. There was nothing in the auditorium. The wooden benches and long narrow tables where we students had sat during ceremonies and assemblies were gone. Only one bench, its back broken, its days of usefulness long past, had been left in the center of the auditorium.

The curtain of the stage had been torn away, and the white-washed wall was exposed to plain view. The piano, the black-board on which the order of the school ceremonies had been written, and all the other paraphernalia had been taken away, and on the lusterless, splintery floor, one dried up rag lay where someone had thrown it. I looked up at the ceiling. The ceiling, lined with narrow boards, was painted pale green. The shade of the green paint, and the grain of the wooden boards, each one 10 centimeters wide, appeared before my eyes, just as they had been thirty years ago. And the milk colored chandelier in the shape of a globe—it was there too, just as it had been.

It was bright inside the auditorium, and perfectly silent. "Makes you sad just to think of it," Hara whispered. "The memorial service," I said, also in a whisper. Oki and Noda nodded in silence. I turned to the stage, naked without its curtain, and gave a silent prayer.

This was the first time I had seen the auditorium since I had graduated. It was neither the memory of school concerts nor of graduation ceremonies that had nailed me to the spot as I stood at the entrance of the auditorium. It was the memory of the ceremony that had been held in October of the year the war ended in memory of the students and teachers who had died in the bombing. The silent prayer I had given was for the spirits of my friends for whom the service had been held. Oki and the others must have been thinking of the same thing. Especially Hara and Oki, for they had had the experience of lying on this auditorium floor, seriously injured after having been exposed to the A-bomb at a munitions factory in Uragami. Hara and Oki, their wounds healed, had both survived, but many other girls had died on this floor under the watchful eyes of teachers and friends. Out of a student body of thirteen or fourteen hundred, nearly three hundred had died between August 9th and the day of the memorial service. Some had been recruited to work in the munitions factories in the Uragami district, and had died instantly there; others had died in their own homes— death had come in various ways. The names of the students were written with a brush on rice paper and put up on the whitewashed wall in four or five rows, each row reaching from one side of the wall to the other.

The homeroom teacher of each class read the names of his or her students. The names of students whose homeroom teacher had been killed in the bombing were read by another teacher of the same grade. As the name of each student was read, there was a stirring among the students who had survived. Then after a while all was quiet, and we sat on the benches, shoulders drooping, as though stupefied. The parents of the students who had died sat along the three walls. The parents were in tears before the memorial service began. The tears turned to sobs, and the sobs drifted steadily toward the center of the room where the students were sitting. "Makes you sad just to think of it," Hara had whispered. Her words plainly expressed the thoughts of that day that had come to life again in each of our hearts. I went into the auditorium and walked over to the window that looked out onto the central school yard. With my back to the window, through which the western sun was shining, I looked at the auditorium once again. Nishida and Oki came over.

Leaning against the low window sill, Nishida said, "I feel so awkward when you talk about the bombing. It makes me feel guilty." Of course, merely hearing the words "memorial service" was enough to tell Nishida what we were thinking about. Nishida had not been exposed to the bombing. Like me, she was a transfer student. She was not one of the "bona-fide" students of N Girls' High School, who had taken the entrance examination after grade school, and been specially chosen to enter. The students of N Girls' High were selected by examination, and they were proud of their school's reputation. They therefore tended to look down on transfer students, even though they were all students of the same N Girls' High. But although we were both transfer students, there was a subtle distinction between Nishida and me.

I entered N Girls' High as a transfer student in March of 1945. On the following August 9th, I was exposed to the A-bomb while working as a labor recruit. Nishida had transferred in October of the year the war ended, on the day of the memorial service. The difference between having been exposed to radiation or not, bore even upon our relationships with Oki and the other "bona-fide" N High girls.

When Nishida said she felt awkward, she was referring to this question of the relationships among us. The distinction between having been exposed or not was what made her feel guilty. Oki laughed and said, "You must be joking! Of course it's better not to have been exposed—that's only natural."

"No, it's not that," said Nishida, "it's not a question of good or bad, it's an emotional thing—emotionally, I want to have been exposed like you." She then went on. "For instance, both you and I were transfer students, so we can't really speak Naga-saki dialect properly, and if we try too hard, it sounds awkward. It's that awkwardness—you know what I mean?" she said to me.

"I still feel it, even now," Nishida continued. "Just now when the four of you were standing at the entrance to the auditorium and you all looked as though you were about to cry. I know what you were thinking about just then—it was the memorial service, wasn't it? But I was thinking of something else." Nishida told us that the scene that had come to her mind was the all school student speech contest that had been held soon after she had transferred to N Girls' High.

"Remember?" Nishida asked me. Around that time I was running a fever from radiation sickness, and stayed at home as much as possible on days when there weren't regular classes. I probably hadn't been at school on the day of the speech con-test. I had no memory of it. "I feel mortified just to think of it!" said Oki, covering her face with her hands in embarrass-ment like a young girl.

"What happened?" asked Hara and Noda, coming over to see what was the matter.

For the contest, each student had been asked to write a speech expounding her views on a topic of her own choosing. The best speech was chosen from each class, and the students chosen to represent their classes delivered their speeches on the stage of the auditorium. It seemed that Nishida and Oki had each been chosen as class representatives, and had thus been rivals for first place in the competition.

Nishida's topic was "On Woman Suffrage," while Oki's was "Careers for Women." In her speech, Oki had vigorously asserted that women should be freed from the task of child bearing, and that was apparently what was making her feel mortified now. "A lucky guess that was—I've never had any children yet," Oki said jokingly. After graduating from a women's university in Tokyo, Oki had come back to Nagasaki, and taken up a career as a junior high school teacher, working for Nagasaki Prefecture. Since then, for no special reason, she had remained single. Expecting to marry someday, she had simply waited, until at last she was over forty.

"But the best place for a woman who doesn't marry is in government service, isn't it?" said Nishida.

"That's right, and besides, you can draw a pension in your old age," added Noda. "Now if my husband dies, I'm out—right then and there," she added, making motions of hanging herself. "Oh no you're not," said Oki, a look of gloom coming over her face.

The problem of education on the outlying islands of Nagasaki Prefecture had recently begun to draw a good deal of public attention. Nagasaki Prefecture has a great number of outlying islands, and the education of the children living on them is a longstanding problem. To Oki, the problem was a most personal one, for it involved the question of whether or not she herself would be assigned to a teaching post on one of the outlying islands. In fact, it seemed very likely that she would be. One of the conditions for taking such a post was that the person be unmarried. Furthermore, during her more than twenty years as a teacher, Oki had never been assigned to a post outside of the city of Nagasaki. Until now, she had been transferred only to junior high schools within the city limits. This was unusual for a teacher in Nagasaki Prefecture, with all its outlying islands. But it was almost certain that she would be ordered to an island post next spring. It wasn't that Oki objected to being transferred. What she was worried about was a recurrence of radiation sickness.

When the list of names of students killed was posted by the school gate immediately after the bombing, the name "Oki" was near the top. Until the day of the memorial service, we had thought that Oki had died after the bombing. The fragments of glass embedded in her arms and back had caused her to lose a lot of blood, and she had lost consciousness from time to time while she was being cared for on the auditorium floor. Carried in the arms of her parents, who had come for her, Oki had gone home, but the way she had looked at that time seems to have been responsible for the theory that she had died. Now she looked healthy enough, but it was as though she was carrying an unexploded bomb around inside her. "As old as I am, I ought to be ready to die, but when it comes right down to it, it's awfully scary," said Oki. There were doctors on the outlying islands, but if radiation sickness was to appear, Oki—I, too, for that matter—wanted to enter the Hospital for Atomic-Bomb Victims in Nagasaki. If we became ill with any kind of disease, we wanted to enter the Hospital for Atomic-Bomb Victims, where the doctors who treated us would have the possibility of radiation sickness in mind. If possible, we wanted to live in a city or town near the Hospital for Atomic-Bomb Victims. Oki's anxiety arose from the thought of crossing the water to some isolated island, separating herself from the Hospital. But a history of exposure to the A-bomb was not acceptable as a reason for refusing a post on one of the outlying islands. Supposing it was—every teacher in Nagasaki Prefecture was probably connected to the bomb in some way. There would be no teachers left to go to the outlying islands. Still, as a fellow A-bomb victim, I could understand Oki's feeling of uncertainty.

"It may sound brutal to say so," Nishida said, "but once you have your plans set, you have to go ahead with them—that's life, isn't it? Even if you are sick."

It's no use standing still in one spot. The present, where we are right now, has always got to be a starting point. That's what Nishida was saying.

Half a year ago, Nishida had lost her husband. He had died

after only two or three days in bed, without so much as a parting word. Fortunately, Nishida had made a name for herself as a fashion designer. Unlike Noda, her husband's death did not mean that she would have to hang herself. Her work had an established reputation, and she seemed to have secured a place for herself in the world of fashion. "You've got to keep going forward no matter what—they're all just waiting to see when you'll trip up," she said. Then she turned to Hara. "Excuse me for being blunt, but are you married?" she asked. Hara shook her head, and answered, "Same as Miss Oki." Compared to Oki, who was rather stout, Hara looked quite sickly.

Her arms and legs were thin, and her face, with its finely chiselled features, like those of a Japanese doll, was a pale, lifeless color. She had been suffering from pernicious anemia since her exposure to the A-bomb, and didn't look as though she could bear up physically under the strain of married life. Oki's parents had died several years ago, one after the other, but Hara's parents were well, and she was living under their care.

"Then the only one of us with a husband is Mrs. Noda," I said. "How about you?" Noda asked me.

"I'm alone," was all I said in answer.

Five of us, once young girls; and now the only one among us who was living a peaceful married life was Noda. Death, divorce, and then Hara and Oki, who had remained single to this day. We stood a while in silence in the spot of sunlight by the window.

"Thirty years; I feel as though I've just been living and that's all," said Hara. "Are we making too much of the bomb?" said Oki in a whisper.

"What about Kinuko? Couldn't she come today?" asked Noda, changing the subject. Oki gave a wild cry. "Oh, I forgot!" Kinuko, who lived in Shimabara, had called Oki that morning. Kinuko knew that Nishida and I were coming from Tokyo for a week's stay in Nagasaki, and she had been planning to come along on today's visit to our alma mater. Then suddenly something had come up, and she hadn't come.

"She'd had her name in for a bed in the A-bomb Hospital. There's an empty bed now, so she said she's going into the hospital tomorrow." At these words of Oki's, Hara furrowed her brow and said, "Radiation sickness?" "No," said Oki, shaking her head, "to have some glass taken out of her back."

Kinuko was an elementary school teacher in Shimabara, in charge of a class of second graders. She had first felt the pain of the fragments of glass in her back during gym class. Kinuko, past forty but still full of energy, was demonstrating a somersault for the children. She had felt it when her rounded back hit the mat—a prickle of pain like the glimmer of an electric light. "I'm getting too old for this sort of thing," she had thought, but nevertheless did another somersault for her pupils. This time, the pain was a sharp one. After school, Kinuko had stopped at the hospital to have it checked. The doctor pressed her back here and there with his fingertips, and then asked Kinuko, "Were you around when the A-bomb was dropped? It might be glass from the time of the bombing, you know." An X-ray was taken, and when they opened her back in one place a week later, they found glass, just as the doctor had said. The skin was hard in that place, and there were several other places like it. They apparently showed up on the X-ray film as shadows. Kinuko was going into the hospital tomorrow for an operation to have all the glass removed, Oki explained.

"Kinuko. I'm not sure I remember her, but wasn't she one of the girls in the speech contest with us?" asked Nishida. "That's right, she was in it," answered Noda. "She was bald then, wasn't she?" It seemed that after the bombing, Kinuko's hair had fallen out, leaving her bald. I had no memory of Kinuko standing bald on the platform in the auditorium, nor did I remember her at all when she was a high school student.

"She talked about the importance of life," Hara remembered. "That's right—her mother and father were killed instantly," said Oki. "Was she an only child?" I asked. "Just like me—a teacher, and all her life alone," said Oki, turning to us with a laugh.

Having no memory of Kinuko as a student, my association with her had begun when we met at a class reunion, or some such sort of meeting. Then, last year, I had seen her for the first time in ten years.

One of our teachers at high school was a young woman named Miss T. Twenty-four or five at the time, she was the daughter of K Temple in Kamimachi in the city of Nagasaki. A graduate of N Girls' High School, she was beautiful; fair skinned, with downy golden hair that shone across her cheeks to her earlobes. Her eyes were bluish-grey, and her chestnut hair was fine; only slightly coarser than a baby's. There are many men and women in Nagasaki who look as though they could be of racially mixed parentage, and Miss T was one of them. Miss T had accompanied the students who had been recruited to work in the munitions factories, and on August 9th, had been killed instantly in the precision machine factory where she and Kinuko had been working.

Having found out that Miss T was buried in the graveyard of K Temple, her birthplace, I had called Kinuko, and in October of last year, we had gone to visit her grave for the first time in the thirty years since her death.

After paying our respects at the grave, we sat down by the roots of the oak tree on the grounds of K Temple, overlooking the city, and talked about our memories of Miss T. Kinuko had been there when Miss T died. She hadn't actually identified the body, but she had witnessed the moment when Miss T, struck in the forehead by the blinding flash, had melted into the light and disappeared. Just at that instant, Miss T had opened her mouth wide, and yelled something to Kinuko. Of course she hadn't been able to hear the words. It might simply have been a scream, but Kinuko had never stopped thinking that somehow she wanted to understand Miss T's last words. She had sketched the shape of those open lips in her mind over and over again, until at last Miss T had become fixed in Kinuko's brain, like a picture stuck fast to a wall.

The burden of the words that she hadn't been able to hear weighed on Kinuko's heart, and lately she had begun to doubt the reality of that scene, even of Miss T's death. She told me that she had come to K Temple to assure herself of the past that was becoming more and more vague in her mind, and to confirm the fact of Miss T's death. "The priest's wife said that they cremated Miss T under this oak tree," she said, citing the words of the priest's wife as proof.

"That's right. The priest's wife was saying that they'd cremated her here," I answered, tapping the gnarled root of the oak tree.

"She said they collected the bones after the cremation. It's best to forget about people who are dead," said Kinuko, tapping the gnarled root as I had done. Just then, Kinuko gave a sharp cry of pain and rubbed the palm of her hand. There was neither blood nor any sign of a wound on the palm of her hand. Puzzled, I asked her if she'd been pricked by a thorn.

"No, glass," she had answered simply. The flatness of Kinuko's words came back to me now.

"You know, the human body's really amazing," Oki said. Four or five years ago, Oki too had had a piece of glass taken out of her back. After the doctor had made the incision, he had removed a lump of fat like a ball of floss silk. Several small fragments of glass, four or five milimeters long, formed the kernel of the fat, and the fat had covered them over like a white, round pearl.

We left the auditorium. Outside the auditorium, the corridor
went off to the right and left with the staircase in the center.
To the right, there were special classrooms. The classrooms we
had used immediately after the war were to the left. As we
walked down the hall, we asked each other which class we had
been in, and who our homeroom teachers had been. The corridor we were walking down formed the base of the U. The
classroom at the corner of the U had only one entrance.

The other classrooms each had a front and a back door. In
the corner classroom, a door had been made in the wall leading
to the classroom next door, in case of emergency. I remembered
the door in the corner classroom. "This was my class," I said to
Nishida. Peeking into the classroom through the window in the
corridor, Nishida asked, "Which one?" Just as she had often
done as a high school girl, Nishida leaned both elbows on the
railing, poked her head and shoulders into the room and looked
around. "This was my class," she said. Nishida too remembered
the doorknob in the wall. Both of our memories of the knob
itself were probably correct, but was the knob we remembered
in the corner classroom, with only one entrance, or in the
classroom on the other side of the wall; the one with the common door? Whichever it was, it seemed certain that my class
and Nishida's had been next to each other.

Nishida and I had been drawn together by the loneliness of
being transfer students, but we had never once been in the
same class. It was strange that we both had memories of the
same classroom.

Oki came up beside Nishida and looked into the room.
"Kinuko was in this class. Were you in the same class?" she
asked me. I said no. Nishida said that she didn't remember
having been in the same class with Kinuko either. "There was
a big hole in this wall," Oki said, walking into the classroom.

Oki remembered everything in detail. Just as in the auditorium, in the semi-darkness of the classroom there were neither chairs nor desks. The blackboard, its surface covered with chalk dust, was hanging on the wall on the corridor side.

This blackboard, which had hung on the side wall of the classroom, had served as a student bulletin board. The door I mentioned earlier was to the right of the blackboard. The hole Oki had referred to was in the wall between the blackboard and the door. The hole was toward the back of the classroom. It was big enough for two high school girls to pass through side by side, and through it we could see what was going on in the classroom next door. When I became bored with my own class, I would turn around and, within the limits of what I could see through the hole, I would wink to my friends in the classroom next door. The hole was soon repaired, but as I traced my memories, it seemed more and more to me as though the corner classroom had been my classroom after all. Because I was short, I had sat in the front of the class. The corner classroom was the only one where you could see into the next room through the hole in the wall from the front seat.

"Remember?" Oki asked. "Remember Kinuko's empty can?" she asked again. "What was she doing with an empty can?" asked Noda.

"You know—she put her mother and father's bones in an empty can and brought it to school with her every day," Oki said. "Ah!" I cried. That girl—was that Kinuko? If it was, then Kinuko and I were classmates. I remembered the girl who came to school with the bones of her parents in her school bag. The girl had kept the bones in a lidless empty can that had been seared red by the flames. To keep the bones from falling out, she had covered the top with newspaper, and tied it with red string. When the girl arrived at her seat, she took her textbooks out of her school bag. Then she took out the empty can, picking it up carefully with both hands, and placed it on the right side of her desk. When classes were over, she would put it back into the bottom of her school bag, again with both hands, and go home. At first, none of us had known what was in the empty can. And the girl did not show any sign of wanting to tell us, either. After our exposure to the A-bomb, the number of things we couldn't talk about openly had increased, so although it weighed on our minds, no one questioned her about it. The love we could see in the girl's fingertips when she handled the can made us feel all the more reluctant to ask.

It had happened during calligraphy class. One day the young calligraphy teacher, who had been discharged from military service and come back, noticed the empty can on her desk. The top of the desk was covered with writing paper, an ink stone, and the textbook.

"What's that can doing there? Put it away in your desk," said the teacher from the platform. The girl hung her head, and held the can on the knees of her workpants. Then, she began to cry. The teacher asked her why.

"It's the bones of my mother and father," the girl answered. The calligraphy teacher took the can from the girl's hands, and placed it in the center of the desk on the platform. "May your parents rest in peace. Let us have a moment of silent prayer in their memory," he said, and closed his eyes. After a long silence, the teacher handed the can back to the girl and said, "After this, leave it at home. Your parents will be waiting there for you. It's better that way."

The girl that day was Kinuko. The incident of the empty can had stayed with me—a pain in the heart, as though an awl had been driven into the midst of my girlhood. It wasn't so much the owner of the can as the incident itself that had made such a deep and lasting impression. The figure of Kinuko as a child, standing in the ruins of her home, bending over to pick up the bones of her mother and father from beneath the white ash, appeared before me in the dim light of the classroom.

Where was that empty can now?

Did Kinuko still keep the bones of her parents in that rusty red can? Was the can on the desk in the room where she lived alone?

Last year, when I had met her at K Temple, Kinuko hadn't mentioned her parents. She had said nothing about her past life or her present life. Perhaps the glass in her back had already begun to hurt around that time.

Kinuko was to enter the hospital tomorrow. How many fragments of glass from thirty years ago would come out of Kinuko's back? What kind of a glow would those smooth white pearls of fat cast when they were brought out into the light?

translated by Margaret Mitsutani

Mitsuharu Inoue

The House of Hands

Nobody's going to marry those Nagasaki girls. Even after they reach marrying age, nobody's going to marry them. Ever since the Bomb fell, everybody's calling them "the never-stop people." And the thing that never stops is their bleeding. Those people are outcasts—damned Untouchables. Nobody's going to marry one of them ever again.

Woman from a rural village in Nagasaki Prefecture

THE grim talk about Seiko Ariie, whose bleeding still hadn't stopped, began shortly after the dealer from Nagasaki had haggled down the price on some Kirimaru dishes. The women unloading firewood at the dock said that Seiko had had a miscarriage in her third month of pregnancy and her bleeding wouldn't stop even though it was ten days ago. The talk was mixed with rumors about a letter that the village office had received from the church in Nagasaki. The letter said that Father Taira would be visiting the village soon to see about fixing up the old House of Hands building. The women brought up this other topic between worried whispers about Seiko, saying that the building was really too dilapidated to be restored. One woman asked if it was true that the House of Hands would be turned into a hospital for T.B. patients with lung disease instead of housing orphans the way it did before the war. But someone else said that couldn't be true because people with T.B. couldn't make pottery and if they didn't make pottery it couldn't be called the House of Hands. Sakie Tomobe broke in to say how worried Seiko's husband, Chikao, must be about his wife.

"Poor Shigeno's babies died after a while, but Seiko's baby wasn't even born!"

"That's right," said Satoko Kirimaru. "Shigeno's first baby lived to be four years old and the second one lasted about eleven days."

"Shigeno wasn't much better."

"But at least her first one lived to four, and the second one survived almost two weeks. Seiko's aren't even going to get born."

"Wonder if the kids'll come again if they reopen the House," said Matakichi as he jumped down from the boat to join the women.

"Well, if they do, I just hope they're better behaved than last time. The ones we had before the war were terrible . . . . But I've got to admit they were cute. Remember when the war got bad and the older kids left to work in the coal mine? Everybody walked the five miles to the dock to see them off."

"I remember that. The older kids always picked on me, but I missed them when they were gone."

"That's right. You were at the House too, weren't you, Matakichi? You're such a good looker now that I'd forgotten what you were like when you were little."

"But if Shigeno's babies didn't make it, and Seiko can't even have babies, then maybe there's no hope for the other two that came to the House with them."

"Just doesn't seem fair. War ended a good fifteen years ago. Why's this have to happen to them now?"

"First Shigeno, and then Seiko—and who knows about Rie and Junko?"

"That long since they came, is it?"

"Rie might be okay. She's a strapping lass."

"It was right after the war. Came by boat, they did."

"Maybe about a year after the war. Anyway, let's get moving. We've got to get back and get unloaded by dark."

Just then, three blasts from a ship's whistle broke through the murky fog that covered the harbor.

"The *Taisho-Maru*. Must be somebody disembarking. He always toots three times when he's got passengers for us."

"Wonder who it is."

"Maybe it's Father Taira."

"Not so soon. He shouldn't be here for another week or so. Was just a couple of days ago the mayor told my dad he was coming in about ten days."

The ship whistled again, impatiently pressing for a reply. As if in response, the dock foreman rushed out of his dock-side store and shouted, "I'm coming." Then to himself as he loosened the mooring rope on the lighter, "Wonder who this could be, unexpected like this."

"Wish I could get on that big ship and go to Nagasaki."

"She's going to Sasebo."

"So Sasebo's good enough. Just want to get out of here."

"Me too," said Satoko quickly.

"Ocean looks a little rough today, doesn't it?"

"You're right. Winter coming on, and they're already winter waves."

"Look! It's two people! Two people getting off."

"Two!"

"Strange that we should have two together."

"Must not be Father Taira then."

"Wonder if they're coming about the pottery."

"Don't know about that, but they're not peddlers. They don't have those big packs like peddlers always have."

Leaving the lighter behind, the *Taisho-Maru* turned toward

the open sea and was gradually lost in the fog, nothing remaining of her but a long wail from her whistle.

"Wonder who they are. Maybe they've come to see the pottery."

"I know! They're doctors—you know, to see Seiko."

"Don't know if there was time to send to Nagasaki for doctors. Just the day before yesterday I heard about her."

"Wouldn't matter if they did. Nothing the doctors can do for her. She's all messed up inside."

"Look! They're not doctors anyway."

As they looked toward the lighter, the dock foreman called out, "Hey, Tanie!"

"What is it?" his wife walked down to the pier's end to hear him better.

"Man here about the Hayashi estate. Go tell the mayor right away."

"Don't see what all the rush is now," she muttered to herself. "Been over a week now since he died. Had the Seventh-day Ceremonies at the Temple just the other day. Oh, well. Maybe it's about the House too."

"So it's not the pottery after all."

"What about the other. . . ."

"Going to the village. Take him along, will you?"

Then they disembarked, one a stiff-looking man in his fifties wearing a heavy jacket over a dark suit and the other one older-looking with his things wrapped up in a bundle. After the first man had left them and gone his way down a side road, the other one asked, "Are you people from Kirimaru?"

"Are you here about the pottery?"

"I would like to go to the village, and I would appreciate it if you would take me along if you are going the same way," he said, a little ill-at-ease.

"All right. You can come with us. But we have to take the firewood," said Matakichi. "It'll be a bit."

"That's okay. I'm in no hurry." His face softened into a smile, and they noticed the crinkles around his eyes.

"Well, I guess we're about ready to go then. Why don't you put your stuff on the cart? It doesn't look heavy enough to make much of a difference."

"Thank you, I believe I will. Teruhide told me it was some way from the port to the village, so I came light, but if you don't mind . . . ." Putting his package on the cart, the man started pushing from behind while Matakichi pulled.

"It's just five miles. It's not too bad if you're used to it, but the hills might be hard walking the first time."

"Who are you going to visit in the village?"

"His name is Wajima—Teruhide Wajima. Perhaps you know him. He teaches there."

"Mr. Wajima! Everybody knows Mr. Wajima."

As they walked beside the cart, Satoko exchanged glances and knowing nods with one of the other women. Their visitor, walking hunched over behind the cart, looked up suddenly at the flicker of movement.

"You're not Rie Nambu, are you?"

"Me? No, not me. But I know her."

"Sorry. I thought you might be Miss Nambu. It was just a feeling I had."

"Are you Mr Wajima's fa . . . a relative of Mr Wajima's or something?"

"Yes, I am. I'm his uncle. Teruhide's father died a long time ago, and I've sort of been responsible for the boy every since. Name's Wajima the same as his. Hatsuma Wajima."

After all of the other people had introduced themselves to Mr. Wajima, Shinobu asked somewhat familiarly, "You from Nagasaki?"

"Shimabara. Work at the farm co-op there."

For a long time, nobody spoke, and the only sound was that of the cart's wheels bumping over the rocky path. As they topped a knoll, Mr. Wajima looked up and commented, "I'll bet there's a great view from here when the weather's right."

"Little windy, though. Get all that wind off the East China Sea. But on a clear day you can see as far as the Goto Islands."

"Do you people always work like this?"

"Not always. We usually work at Satoko's dad's pottery," Shinobu said, with a nod in Satoko's direction. "But everybody helps gather firewood for the kiln. Not that busy now, so most of the men stayed home today, but . . . ."

"So this is to fire the kiln, is it?"

"But this isn't all. We usually make two trips a day with two carts."

"So you're . . . ."

"And Rie works for my father," Satoko said with a sudden burst of pent-up words.

"Satoko, hold your tongue," one of the other women scolded.

"Oh, my. What have I started?" Mr. Wajima said, putting his hand to his mouth in an apologetic gesture that started Shinobu giggling and soon had the other women joining in as well.

"Oh, dear, I hope I haven't gotten anybody into any trouble," he added with a loud chuckle.

"Oh, no. Rie's a really pretty girl."

"I hear she's been brought up at the pottery—sorry, by your folks—ever since her parents passed away."

"That's right. Ever since she came to the House of . . ." Satoko broke off in mid-sentence, appalled by what she had blurted out as a voice kept ringing in her mind: "Seiko's bleeding hasn't stopped yet."

"What's that?"

"To her parents' house, that is," one of the other women hastily tried to repair the damage.

"I hear she comes from sturdy stock."

"Yes, strong and handsome, Rie is."

But even as they were saying this, Shinobu was thinking about what Satoko had said earlier down at the dock about how Shigeno's babies didn't make it, Seiko's didn't even get born, and maybe there was no hope for the other two girls Rie and Junko.

"Sky's turning a little darker. Better hurry," someone said, and the group fell silent again as the cart rolled along the rude path.

"Oh to be young again," Mr. Wajima said in a voice that sounded oddly out of place.

*　　　*　　　*

The talk about Mr. Wajima's uncle's coming to Kirimaru to see Rie spread throughout the village, and by noon the next day there wasn't a single person at the pottery who didn't know about it.

"Hope everything works out all right. Seems like a nice enough person. But be sure never to tell him about the House of Hands," everybody added, just to be sure.

Seiko heard the story from Shigeno, who came to call soon after the sick woman's husband had left for his job at the pottery.

"Don't be too hard on yourself. You're still young. You can have kids anytime," she said, stroking Seiko's pale cheek.

"I must look terrible."

"You'll be better soon. I brought you a carp in the creel. It's still alive, so I ran some water in the sink and put it in there. You can eat it later. Be good for you. Where's your mom?"

"She's out. Did you bleed bad after you had your second one?"

"Pretty bad, but I got over it with a special concoction of burdock, pomegranate, and carp blood. Nothing we could do for the kids, though. They just died. It was God's will," she said with a tightening of her jaw.

"What about Juro? How'd he take it when the kids died?"

"Him? He's . . . resigned himself to it. Just the other day he said we should talk to the Father the next time he comes."

"Talk to the Father? What about?"

"About adopting a child. Kids'll come if they reopen the House, and since we can't have any of our own, we're thinking of adopting one. I want a little girl."

"Maybe none of us can."

"What do you mean? I'm just talking about myself. You're still young, and you can have kids anytime. You're going to be fine just as soon as we get this bleeding stopped."

"I'm sorry. Could you make yourself some tea? . . . But you know how everybody talks. The four girls who came to the House together, and we all got white blood, and . . . ."

"Whoever said that? Maybe me, but I'm just one of us. And look at Rie and Junko. There's nothing wrong with them! And we don't even know what caused your miscarriage. Really, miscarriages happen all the time. They can happen to anyone. If you want to know, the gossip had it that you had a miscarriage because Chikao loves you too much."

"Yes, I know. His . . . my mother told me," Seiko said dryly. "And she said that since yours died so quickly, if it turns out that I can't have children, then nobody'll want to marry Rie or Junko."

"Well, she was wrong. Rie's going to get married. In fact, Mr. Wajima's uncle came yesterday to make the arrangements. And you can tell her I said so."

"Rie's getting married? To Mr. Wajima?"

"Right. Rie's going to marry Mr. Wajima. And that leaves only Junko, and you know what a high-spirited girl she is. I can't imagine her not getting married."

"Really, Rie's getting married?"

"How I envy these young people. They can marry whoever

they want to."

"What? Didn't you want to marry Juro?"

"Actually, I had my eye on somebody else, but everything happened so fast. It was just a month after he came back from the war. I was married before I knew it," she said with a laugh.

"But Rie . . . is Rie going to be okay?"

"What do you mean?"

"Well, even if she gets married, what if she can't have children? What if somebody finds out that . . . ?"

"Quit your worrying. Mr. Wajima—the teacher—he knows all about the House of Hands. That's how they met."

"What about his uncle? I hope he doesn't find out about me."

"He won't. Nobody at the pottery's going to tell him anything."

"But if Mr. Wajima . . . ."

"He won't. He loves Rie too much to say anything stupid."

"I wonder if it's true all four of us from the House really did get white blood," mused Seiko.

"Nonsense. I don't know if our blood is white or what, but all four of us have been fine for over a decade. So stop worrying and start getting well again."

"I've been thinking."

"About?"

"About when we came to the House. You know, when you led Rie and me up the hill with Father Taira, five miles on foot all the way from the dock. Remember? Even though the war was over, there still wasn't much food. I remember that. And I remember the way we cried ourselves to sleep at night, huddled together with our faces turned toward Nagasaki."

"I'd forgotten. I started working at the pottery almost right away. But you were only five or six then, weren't you? Must have been tough. Things weren't any easier at the pottery though. People bossing one around and telling me the House had a different religion. Said they were Cryptos* and we were different. I didn't understand what they meant until Mr. Kirimaru explained it to me."

"I still don't understand it," Seiko said, starting to get up.

"Where do you think you're going? You're not supposed to get up."

"Bathroom," Seiko said with obvious effort.

"Well, okay, but let me help you."

"It's okay. I can manage by myself." Picking a sanitary napkin from the box by her bedding, she stumbled unsteadily down to the dirt hall and off to the bathroom. Watching her, Shigeno remembered what Juro had said to her the other day. "I don't mind so much for myself, but what's Chikao going to do? It's going to be tough on his family if they can't have kids. Chikao's an only child, you know, and if Seiko's childless that's the end of the line. It's bad enough for us, but I've got lots of brothers who can have kids to carry on the family name. We can shrug it off, but not Chikao. It's all the talk. Even old Shichi told me today when we banked the fire at the kiln, 'I know miscarriages happen, but I've never heard of this bleeding disease. Maybe the girls the Father brought to the House are all the same. You know what I mean, don't you? After all, Shigeno's your wife.' I can't believe he said it," and Juro had clicked his tongue in disgust.

"Still pretty bad," Seiko said as she tottered back.

"Can't figure it out."

"Mr. Saijo from the village office comes every day to give me a shot. He used to be a medic during the war, and he says I'll be okay if I just stay in bed."

"Maybe you should make yourself a broth of sweet creeper. Might work, and it couldn't do any harm," Shigeno said with an affectionate touch to Seiko's shoulder that drew only a sigh of despair in return.

"Tired?"

"Starting to get me down."

"Why don't you get some sleep then? I'll be back later."

"You know, what you said a while ago . . . ."

"About what?"

"You know, about how the Kirimaru villagers' religion is different from the House. I asked the Father about it once, and he says it's not true. But I don't know. I get confused sometimes. Chikao doesn't say anything, but mother sometimes gets on my nerves about it. I wanted to spend some time talking with you about it."

"Then hurry up and get well, and we'll have lots of time to talk. I don't really know that much about it myself. All I know is what Mr. Kirimaru told me," Shigeno said as she stood up to leave. "Take care of yourself. I'll be back to see you again real soon."

*   *   *

In a room over the shop, Hiroyuki Kirimaru recalled with irritation what the dealer from Nagasaki had said: "I was really struck when I discovered your father's Crypto pottery in that old second-hand shop. I know things are different now, and you have to keep up with the times, but you really should stick to Crypto pottery if you can. If you could just make it like you used to . . . ." Then he had left after taking advantage of Hiroyuki's desperation to knock down the price of the dishes he bought. And then there was that business with Kunisada. "One of those days when nothing goes right."

"What's that, father?" asked Satoko from the kitchen where she was doing the lunch dishes.

"Nothing."

"He came because of Rie, didn't he?"

"Who? Oh, him. Yes." But in fact, Hiroyuki was more concerned with what Kunisada had said than with this uncle of Wajima's who had shown up just after lunch.

"And he asked you to give Mr. Wajima Rie's hand in marriage, didn't he?"

"Sort of," he answered his daughter absently as he thought about what Kunisada had said: "Sir, I have a matter to discuss with you."

"Yes, what is it, Kunisada? But why don't you come in and we can talk about it in here?"

"Thank you, sir. We . . . I understand that . . . somebody's coming from Nagasaki . . . and that they're going to rebuild the House of Hands. Of course, there have been rumors like this for some time, but this is more certain because the . . . from Nagasaki . . . ." Kunisada hedged, trying to avoid mentioning Father Taira by name.

"You're right that somebody's coming. But that doesn't mean they're going to rebuild the House. The mayor just told me Father Taira's coming to look at the building and see what kind of shape it's in."

"Well, some of the men have been talking about this, and we . . . that is, the priest at Shokoji Temple says we don't want to make a big fuss about it, and so he suggested . . . ."

"He suggested what?"

"Well, we wanted to see how you felt about it before things got out of hand, so they asked me to come see you."

"Felt about what?"

"Well, the priest says Cryptos should stay Crypto, and we . . . ."

"Not understanding what Kunisada was driving at, Hiroyuki had felt as though he were slipping into quicksand.

From the kitchen, his daughter's voice broke into his thoughts.

"When are Rie and Mr. Wajima getting married?"

"What's that?"

"Father, you haven't heard a word I've been saying," she said with a quiet laugh to herself.

"And if the House is rebuilt, they'll build a church too. And we can't be Cryptos if there's a church here. At least that's what the priest from the temple says. Even though the House was built before the war, thanks to the war . . . I really shouldn't say thanks to the war, but . . . with the war it was practically closed and things got back to normal. But now if we let them renovate the House, they'll want to build a church too, and then how can we still be Cryptos?" And then, seemingly going off on a different tangent, he continued. "Of course, after we lost the war and Nagasaki got blown up we thought it wouldn't be right to turn the orphans away. But now . . . ."

"But the House was built a long time ago, back when our fathers decided we shouldn't be Cryptos any more and okayed the approach from the church in Nagasaki."

"But then we got to thinking, and as the years went by, we realized that these kids were orphaned by the people who dropped the Bomb, and *they* should take care of them, so there's no reason the House should be rebuilt now."

"Look, let's not be rash about this. Sure, this village was Crypto for a long time, but we decided to return to the church in our fathers' time. And besides, the church in Nagasaki owns the House anyway, and we have no right to stop them if they want to rebuild it. It's their House." And then, feeling somewhat put out by Kunisada's argument, he added, "Besides, the young people don't really care about being Cryptos nowadays anyway."

"I know the young ones make light of our faith, but the fact is our fathers gave it up and accepted the Nagasaki church only under duress. That's what the old people say. It's because the church in Nagasaki helped us before the war, when the pottery was almost bankrupt, so how could we refuse them? But we're still Cryptos at heart. That's why no church has been built after all these years."

"Under duress or not, we did return to the church, and we can't stop the Father from coming."

"But we've been Cryptos for hundreds of years. The priest at Shokoji says our ancestors would never forgive us if we quit—not after Shimabara."

Implying that he understood Kunisada's feelings but regarded the matter as settled, Hiroyuki took a deep breath and fell silent.

"Besides, the House of Hands is cursed," Kunisada said with a sudden vehemence.

"Is what?"

"Cursed. That's why the girls who were raised at the House can't stop their bleeding once it starts."

"That's got nothing . . . ."

"That's what the elders say. It's not only the Bomb. It's a curse because we've turned our backs on the old religion."

"Father, what should I take Seiko?" Satoko startled him out of his reverie.

"She still bleeding?"

"She could hardly even open her mouth when Rie saw her this morning. I'm going to go see her tonight."

"Hmmm."

All of a sudden, in the inner part of the workshop, Kunisada's potting wheel started whirling again.

"Father, tell me what happened about Rie. What did Mr. Wajima's uncle say?" Finished with the dishes and wiping her hands, Satoko came into Hiroyuki's room.

"Oh, yes. Could you ask Rie to come in here?" Hiroyuki said as though the thought had just occurred to him.

"Rie! My father wants to see you right away!" Opening the door to the workshop, Satoko called out in a festive tone.

*   *   *

"I don't understand why I can't tell your uncle about the House of Hands. Mr. Kirimaru told me to say I was at the pottery ever since my parents died. Why's that? I'm not ashamed of being from the House."

With a "Shhh," Teruhide hushed Rie.

"Don't talk so loud. He's right up there," he said, pointing a warning finger toward his room just above the playground.

"What will your uncle say when he sees me?" It was the same question Rie had asked so many times before.

"Let's wait a while," he said, steering her toward the monkey bar.

"Dark tonight, isn't it? Sky looks like a coat of black paint."

"Just be sure you don't tell him anything about the House, okay? It's all right if I know, but not him."

"I still don't understand. But if you insist, I won't say a word."

"This is really a strange village," Teruhide said, dropping out of the local dialect into a more detached and scholarly tone. "The people are Crypto-Christians, but a lot of them are Buddhist too, and they've turned against the Christian church. Maybe they've gotten their religions all mixed up after pretending to be Buddhist for such a long time."

"But I'm not Crypto."

"I know, but you were brought up by them," he mused.

"No I wasn't. I was raised in the House. The House isn't Crypto. The House was built by the orthodox Catholic church in Nagasaki. They sent relief goods, and people to help."

"You know," he said, slipping back once more into the Kirimaru dialect, "I hear Catholics can only marry Catholics."

"Maybe other Catholics, but not House Catholics. We're different."

"Well, maybe you used to be different. But not now. Now a Father's coming from Nagasaki, and maybe we won't be able to get married after all."

"Wonder if he'll say anything. But Shigeno and Seiko are married to Crypto men," Rie said pensively.

"Well, Shigeno and Seiko got married when there was no Father here, but maybe in our case . . . ."

Catching the hint of tease in his tone, Rie quickly slapped out at him as he laughed and ducked away.

"House of Hands. Sure is a funny name," he said after a while, taking her hand in his.

"There's a House of Hands in the mountains in northern Italy with a pottery where priests and believers make pots and dishes. A priest in Nagasaki named this one after it. Father Ōno named it when the village returned to the faith from being Cryptos."

"You sure do know a lot about it. I'd never heard that before."

"Wonder if your uncle's going to like me?"

"Sure he will. How could he not like you?"

"Then tell me why I can't tell him about the House? If you tell a lie, you've got to keep telling it forever and ever."

"If you tell him about the House, then he'll know when you four came to Kirimaru."

"So what's wrong with that?"

"And then if he finds out about Shigeno, he'll start putting two and two together and making five. He's really old-fashioned."

"He'd probably find out about Seiko, too," Rie said in a voice tight with anxiety.

"I understand, but my uncle might not."

"Let's go then. I don't know what your uncle's going to say, but let's get it over with."

"Just don't mention the House, okay?"

"I might be a bleeder like Seiko, you know. We might not be able to have any children either," she said, turning away.

"Back where I come from, nobody wants to marry anyone from Nagasaki. That's why I don't want you telling him about the House," he said, holding her firmly by the shoulders.

"But he'll find out I'm from Nagasaki anyway, and he'll find out about the House too soon enough!"

"Nobody's going to tell him. He knows you're from Nagasaki, but I told him you were evacuated here during the war."

Resigned but uneasy, she said, "Still, I don't like it. Don't you know it's a sin to tell a lie?" And then a short while later to herself, "And I'm so worried about Seiko."

*　　　*　　　*

"Uncle Hatsuma, I brought Rie," Teruhide called out in lieu of knocking at his own door.

"Well, come in then. A Mrs. Kato came by a little while ago and left these," Hatsuma said, not looking at Rie as he opened the door.

Glancing at the table, Teruhide saw a large bottle of home-brewed sake and a pot of stew. "She didn't have to do that."

"So you're Rie?"

"How do you do. My name is Rie Nambu." By this time, Rie was sitting formally with her legs tucked under her, and she bowed deeply from this position.

"Please don't stand on formalities. Make yourself comfortable."

"Thank you, sir."

"Well, let's talk business later. It would be a shame to keep this good sake waiting." So saying, Teruhide put three cups on the table. "You want some too, Rie?"

"None for me, thank you," she replied hesitantly.

"Teruhide wrote saying he was bringing you home for the New Year's holidays. Of course, that would make everything final, so I thought I'd just stop by and get to know you first myself. Taking a bride is not quite the same thing as adopting a kitten, you know," he added, tossing down his sake quickly.

"Yes, sir," Rie said.

"Rie, why don't you make yourself comfortable?" Teruhide urged.

"The boy's father died when he was still quite young, and I've been a father to Teruhide ever since." After a brief pause, "He's told me almost everything about you. Nineteen, aren't you?"

"Yes, I'm going to be nineteen soon."

"Hmmm, that makes eight years' difference. Just right." He took another cup of sake.

"She's a very hard worker," Teruhide interjected.

"The boy graduated from Teachers' College, and I don't think he should stay at this country school all his life. Sooner or later, he'll come back to Shimabara. Think you'd be able to leave the village?"

"Of course, once we're married, I would go wherever he went."

"Well, nothing personal, but there are some Crypto communities that don't let anybody leave. Never can be too sure."

"But I'm not Crypto."

"Oh, yes, Mr. Kirimaru told me about that. I understand your parents were killed by the Bomb in Nagasaki after you'd been evacuated here. At least, that's what Teruhide told me."

"What did Mr. Kirimaru say about Rie's quitting her job at the pottery to get married?" Teruhide asked, cutting in to change the subject.

"Oh, he seemed very pleased about the engagement. Said he hoped she'd work at the pottery as long as you're in Kirimaru, but he knows young people have their own lives."

"He's a real gentleman, Mr. Kirimaru is, isn't he?" Teruhide said.

"But don't you have any other relatives, Miss Nambu? Isn't there anyone else you should talk this over with besides Mr. Kirimaru?"

"No, sir, no one."

"She was brought up at the Kirimarus' since she was little."

"This is pretty strong sake," Hatsuma declared, putting his cup down with a thump.

"Sure you don't want any, Rie?" Teruhide urged.

"No thank you," she demurred.

"Pretty potent stuff. A-ha-ha."

Just then, a women outside called out loudly, "Mr. Wajima! Mr. Wajima!"

"Who's there! What is it?" Teruhide asked, opening the window.

"It's me. Satoko Kirimaru."

"Satoko?" asked Rie standing up quickly.

"Is that you, Rie? You'd better come quick. Seiko's gotten worse."

"Oh, no!"

"Hurry. Everybody's there."

"What about the doctor?" Teruhide asked.

"Matakichi's gone to get him. I wanted Rie to know before it's too late."

"If you will excuse me, sir . . . ." Rie said, taking her leave with a bow to Teruhide's uncle.

"Somebody sick, huh?" Hatsuma inquired of nobody in particular. And then after Rie and Satoko had left, "Wonder what it is."

"Doctor lives quite a long way off," Teruhide volunteered.

*   *   *

As the men and women crowded around where Seiko lay, one of the women peering in from the outer room asked of nobody in particular, "Why'd she take a turn for the worse all of a sudden?"

"Must have lost a lot of blood."

"It was all so sudden, this . . . ." and then she stopped as Satoko and Rie rushed in breathlessly.

"Hurry up. Shigeno and Junko are already with her."

Satoko sat down with the other women as Rie went into the room where Seiko lay. Chikao turned and greeted Rie solemnly. "Thank you so much for coming."

"What happened?" Rie asked, looking at Seiko as she lay with her eyes closed.

"I found her unconscious in the bathroom when I got back from the bath this evening," he answered.

"She wasn't that bad when I came around noon," Shigeno added.

"What's taking the doctor so long?" Junko asked impatiently.

"We should have taken her to the doctor's long ago. I'd heard she was sick, but I didn't realize she was this bad," Hiroyuki said remorsefully.

"Don't go blaming yourself for what's not your fault, Mr. Kirimaru," Chikao said.

"Because of her miscarriage," Chikao's mother said, but it was not clear if she meant they should have taken her to the doctor's because of her miscarriage or that there had not seemed to be any reason to call the doctor because it was only a miscarriage.

"We've been giving her shots to stop the bleeding, and I didn't . . . didn't think she was this bad, and . . . ." said Chikao.

"Water," Seiko asked with a faint movement of her head.

"Okay," Shigeno said, looking at Chikao to make sure it was all right to give her some.

Swallowing a sip of water, Seiko asked, "Rie?"

"Yes, here I am. How are you feeling?"

"Hear you have a visitor," Seiko said almost inaudibly.

"What?"

"Your visitor," Shigeno amplified. "Mr. Wajima's uncle."

"Don't make her talk too much," Hiroyuki fretted.

". . . or about Shigeno . . . ."

"What's that?" Shigeno moved closer to Seiko to be able to hear her better.

"Don't tell him about me or Shigeno," Seiko repeated faintly.

"She means Rie," Junko explained.

"Seiko!" shouted Chikao, trying to rouse his wife.

"Saijo! Do something!" called Hiroyuki to the former medic in the next room.

". . . or the House or . . . ."

"Seiko!" screamed Shigeno as Seiko fell silent.

Hearing Shigeno's cry, Satoko rushed in from the next room.

"Seiko! Seiko! Say something! Seiko!" called Chikao as he shook her limp body.

"Girl's dead," muttered Saijo disinterestedly.

"Shut up!" Hiroyuki snapped at him.

"Seiko! Who needs children anyway? Seiko! Answer me!" shouted Chikao as he pounded his fist on the floor.

At this, the women rushed in from the next room and began sobbing.

"She's been called," Hiroyuki pronounced.

"She's been called! She's been called!" the chorus went up from the wailing women as they clasped their hands in prayer.

With bowed heads, Shigeno and Junko made the sign of the cross. Hiroyuki looked at them uneasily and hesitantly clasped hands in an ambivalent gesture.

"She's been called," said Chikao as he too clasped his hands in prayer.

"Save us, merciful Buddha!" Chanting a Buddhist invocation, Chikao's mother glared at Shigeno and Junko, who continued crossing themselves.

"She's been called. Earth to earth, ashes to ashes," said Hiroyuki.

"She's been called! She's been called!"

"Amen," from Rie and Junko.

"No girls from the House ever going to get married again," Ine suddenly burst out.

"Mother! How can you say such a thing!" Chikao demanded angrily. "Don't you dare say another word."

"It's a retribution! Because they . . . ."

"Ine, don't talk like that! We're all the same, the House Christians and the Crypto-Christians," Hiroyuki admonished.

"There's been nothing but unhappiness ever since those girls came to Kirimaru. My poor Chikao."

Moving closer to Rie, Shigeno whispered, "Don't forget Seiko's last words. Don't ever say anything about Seiko and me or the House to . . . ."

"The funeral will be tomorrow at one. Spread the word. Shigeno, Junko, Rie, you stay here . . . ." said Hiroyuki, taking charge of the arrangements.

"No! Nobody from the House stays for a wake in *my* house!" screamed Ine.

"Stop it!" Chikao shouted.

"We don't want to upset the arrangements now, do we?" said one of the other women, trying to calm Ine.

"Besides, Seiko's spirit would be lonely without Rie here," added Satoko.

"It'd be bad if Mr. Wajima's visitor found out about Seiko."

"Don't anybody say anything about the House."

"I don't care if he does find out. I haven't done anything wrong," cried Rie.

"There's no difference between the House people and us. I want that understood," Hiroyuki said firmly.

"If they stay, I'm leaving. Oh, what's to become of my poor Chikao?" Ine said between loud sobs.

At that moment, Kunisada and another craftsman from the pottery came in, heads bowed. "We heard Seiko's taken a turn for the worse."

"She's just been called," Chikao told them.

"I'm sorry."

"She's been called."

"And *they* said for those House girls to stay for the wake," Ine complained to Kunisada.

"Seiko was worried about Rie until the very last. So I decided to have Shigeno, Rie, and Junko stay. After all, they grew up together," Hiroyuki explained somewhat defensively.

"It's true Seiko was from the House, but she was Chikao's family, too," retorted Kunisada defiantly. But then he added, "But I guess there's nothing we can do about it if it's already settled."

"Seiko's been called to save our souls," Hiroyuki recited, and the women wailed, "She's been called. She's been called," Ine's sobs drowning out Junko's "Amen."

*　　　*　　　*

Watching the flames as they noisily devoured Seiko's coffin, Rie wanted to cry out. "She died after telling me not to say anything about Shigeno or herself. She never said another word after that. To the very last, she was worried about Teruhide and me."

The flames that consumed Seiko's body seemed to echo Teruhide's words just before the funeral. "We're in trouble. I don't know who told him, but my uncle found out about the House. I can apologize for not having told him from the very beginning, but nobody where I'm from wants to marry somebody from Nagasaki."

Seiko became part of the roaring flame, and Rie threw her reply to Teruhide into the hot blaze. "And what's that supposed to mean—that he won't let us get married because I'm from the House?" "Well, he didn't come right out and say it, but things don't look so good for us. Wonder who told him." "He would have found out anyway, even if nobody'd told."

Seiko seemed to leap up within the blaze, and her words came to Rie again. "Don't tell him about how Shigeno lost her babies and how I'm bleeding, or about the House. You'll never be able to get married if you do."

Then it was over, and Kunisada was addressing Mr. Kirimaru

in front of the assembled pottery workers. "Can't you do something to stop the church in Nagasaki from rebuilding the House? There'll be a lot more kids coming if they do. Don't you see? We've had enough trouble with these four. They can't have babies and they won't stop bleeding. Any more come and this'll be a village of Untouchables. None of our women will ever be able to marry outside of Kirimaru.

"Cryptos've got to stay Cryptos. We've seen what happens when the old religion is defiled. Now there's a rumor that Junko'll never be able to get married. I feel sorry for the poor girls, but things'll just get worse if we let them rebuild the House. Junko won't be the only one. Let them rebuild, and we'll have a whole village of kids from Nagasaki with their bodies all bombed out. The word'll get out that Kirimaru's a village of bleeders, and we'll be a village of outcasts, unable to marry outside Kirimaru. We'll be a village of Untouchables. Nobody'll ever . . . ." Kunisada's voice rose, flowing like oil fueling Seiko's funeral pyre.

translated by Frederick Uleman and Kōichi Nakagawa

Crypto-Christians Bands of Christians who practiced their faith in secret after the Tokugawa Shogunate banned Christianity and decisively crushed the Christian forces at Shimabara in 1637–38. In seeking to protect their secrecy, they developed a distinctly cryptic form of Christianity often overlaid with the trappings of Buddhism.

Hiroko Takenishi

The Rite

To the riverside house with the tin roof on which several bunches of red chili peppers had been set out to dry they brought at evening an injured man, stretched out on a wooden shutter. By the entrance to the small dirt-floored front area stood two pickling tubs with big stone weights on the lids, casting long shadows in the westerly sun. The hill that pressed in on the house from behind was fully exposed to the late sunlight, so that even the texture of its soil showed clearly. Holding the shutter front and rear were two sturdy young men with towels around their necks and split-toed tabi sneakers on their feet. The doorway was so narrow there was no way they could get in. They appeared to be talking about it and trying to figure out what to do. The injured man's head was thickly bandaged and from under the thin quilt that covered his body, his gaitered legs stuck out, also shod with tabi sneakers. The goings-on beyond the river were so unusual that Aki couldn't tear herself away from the lattice window. Her school satchel, flap open, lay there unheeded by her side.

A middle-aged woman emerged from the front room. It was the woman who washed rice and rinsed clothes every day at the river. Crying in a shrill voice, she clutched at the injured man, and then throwing her arms in the air and screaming something at the top of her voice, she ran to the next house some distance away. Between there and the next house was a rough log cabin that looked like some sort of storage shed. At the foot of the hill the only inhabited buildings were the woman's house and the house next door that she had run to. Both were roofed with tin, and judging by their size, other than the dirt-floored front area, there couldn't be more than one room worth calling a room.

Soon the woman hurried back from the next house, bringing an old woman with her. The door panel had been removed and now, the makeshift stretcher slid easily inside. The injured man must be the husband who came home drunk late every night, thought Aki. The woman who ran to the neighboring house must be the wife, and the one she brought back with her must be the mother of one of them. The two young men leaned over the injured man and peered into his face. Three small children had climbed on top of the quilt and seemed to be patting and stroking the injured man. When one of the children slithered off the quilt and wandered away, the other two did the same, and then all three left the house.

Already dusk was closing in. The three children each started picking up pebbles, and then together, facing the stream, they began seeing who could throw the farthest.

That night, mingling with the river noises, there came to Aki's ears a low sound of crying. But it grew steadily louder and there was no sign that it would ever stop. And as Aki opened the shutters a little to try to see what was happening beyond the river, the thought struck her that now, under that naked electric light over there, a man's death was drawing near. Was it through his own carelessness he got hurt, she wondered, or had he been attacked by someone? And those people left behind, how would they be able to live now?

Aki remembered when that house was built. One day a man and a woman and three children came to the riverside with a pushcart full of lumber and sheets of tin. They chose a site at the foot of the hill and drove stakes into the ground. First of all, they built the little log cabin. Then they built one house with a tin roof. All day long the man swung his hammer and wielded his saw; the children romped and raced around; the wife washed vegetables in the river. Then, when the second house was finished, the old woman appeared from somewhere and took up her abode there. It was shortly after this that the man started going out every day, dressed in a workman's happi coat, his legs in gaiters and tabi sneakers on his feet, and then, more and more often, he could be heard late at night, singing off key in a loud voice. The man had a slurred pronunciation that jarred the ear, but this was not simply because he was drunk. The woman's speech too, and even the way the children talked, were quite different from Aki's own manner of speaking.

The day after the injured man was brought home and the day following that, the dried red peppers were left where they were on the roof. The hearse that Aki thought must surely come to that house in the end did not come after all. All she saw was a canvas covered pushcart, escorted by the two women and the three children and several brawny looking men, going slowly along the road by the river.

From the far off days of her childhood, long before Aki had ever experienced such things as the sickness or death of her own flesh and blood, that was a funeral that stayed like a weight on her mind.

There's lightning flashing!

Aki wakes up with the feeling she has just come out of a queer disturbing dream. She seems to have woken up in the middle of her own scream. With her mind on this, Aki gropes for the switch of the bedside lamp. Finds it. Presses it. There is the familiar ceiling of her four-and-a-half-mat rented room. It is just after two in the morning. In the dusty vase, the fresh summer flowers she had put there only yesterday are already wilted and drooping. By her bed a weekly magazine, a cigarette case, a lighter, an ashtray.

From time to time the wind rustles the branches of the trees and bushes. Aki turns over and lies face down, lights a cigarette, inhales.

Pictured on the cover of the weekly that Aki had bought yesterday at the subway station entrance was the lid of a jar. When she left the construction company where she worked, she walked along the pavement that her heels always caught in, to the shop run by a German near the subway station. Often on Saturday afternoons Aki would come to this shop for a late lunch of tea and pie. She had done so yesterday. And then, to buy a weekly, she had gone to the station newsstand at the side of the ticket window. While she was looking for one with an interesting cover, her hand, as though it were the natural thing to do, reached for the one with that lid.

Except for the magazine's title, the whole cover was taken up by the face of a young Egyptian nobleman, drawn big against a vermillion background. When Aki learned that this was the lid of an urn used in ancient Egypt as a container for the viscera of corpses to be mummified, a strange thrill ran through a corner of her heart. It was as if she alone in the midst of a multitude was experiencing a secret joy, but this joy was overshadowed by a heavy, helpless gloom. "There's someone watching me!" Suddenly Aki had this uneasy feeling and looked up, shifting her gaze in the direction of the ticket gate.

A young man approaching and a woman, turning her back on him without a word, and going out to the sidewalk. A man in a sudden outburst of anger at a woman who appeared to have come late for their date. A group of girl students, each hand in hand with a friend, their free hands separately hailing a taxi. A plump middle-aged woman approaching with rapid mincing steps. Every face looking totally intent on some immediate, intimate aim. Relieved, Aki lifted up the handbag on her arm and went through the ticket gate onto the platform. She sat down on an empty bench, and then resumed her examination of the urn lid.

The nobleman had a wig and his eyes were of obsidian and quartzite. According to the explanation, a glass image of the sacred serpent had originally been attached to the forehead. His loved ones left behind would have assembled before him to mourn this dead man. Some would have prayed, some would have waved incense censers, some would have made funeral offerings of great price. The lid of the alabaster urn would then have been removed and his internal organs gently placed within. What memories would have stirred then in those people as lid met jar again?

There without a doubt was a fitting way to start out on death's journey, with the dead well tended and watched over by the living. Thinking of that man who had left behind a part of his own flesh, and his people who had taken it into their keeping, in what was surely a most dignified and solemn ceremony, it seemed to Aki that there indeed was a secure and reassuring way to die.

It was three days now since she had gone to the suburb where Tomiko lived in front of the station, carrying Tomiko's postcard asking for help in her handbag.

Tomiko's house had a little shop in it that sold the latest books and magazines, along with cigarettes. Whenever a train stopped at the station, a couple of customers would drop in at the shop. Although it was a hot sticky evening, Tomiko was there minding the shop, dressed in a maternity smock that was a little on the long side. The moment she caught sight of Aki, she let out a sudden cry of joy and grabbed her by the arms. It had been four or five years since they had last met. Watching Tomiko's friendly, darting eyes, Aki thought,

"She's just the same as ever!"

"I want to have the shop remodelled. I've been telling my husband all along that when it came time for that, I'd call on your place."

The husband in question did not put in an appearance. For Aki, it was not that Tomiko's request was in any way unusual, but willy-nilly she had to bear in mind the likely reaction of her section chief, who much preferred new jobs to remodelling. Anyway, Aki got most of the necessary data for the estimate from her friend and briskly wrote it down. There was nothing further she needed to be told. At this point Tomiko said, "My husband is still on his rounds. Anyway, that's what we want. Please do the best you can for us!" Aki said she needed about a week.

"Sure! That's fine!"

Then Tomiko bowed formally from the waist and that was the end of the business talk.

A boy's voice was saying the conventional "Excuse me for eating first! That was a good meal!" The boy had come out from under the door curtain of a side door that seemed to communicate with the kitchen, and now with lowered head, was standing facing Tomiko.

Who does that remind me of! thought Aki.

The moment of confusion, then the self-conscious look on the boy's face! That was the face that Noboru had often shown her when he was late for a date. With his nervous temperament, he was such a stickler for punctuality that whenever he was late, Aki used to wonder uneasily if she herself hadn't made a mistake. "I got caught by the prof."—that's all he would say as he sat down, so boyishly that sometimes Aki found it hard to believe that Noboru was older than she. If Aki asked Noboru a question about the university research laboratory where he worked, he would answer in great detail, but he never took the initiative in talking about himself or his work. Whenever

Aki came late, Noboru would immediately start telling her about what he had been reading while waiting, and before she could even apologize for being late she would be drawn into Noboru's conversation, and as often as not they would soon be deep in talk about something else altogether.

"Why don't you eat supper here with me before you go!" Invited thus by Tomiko, Aki walked under the door curtain. More than ten years had gone by since they had graduated together from the same girls' school. Aki had never once met Tomiko's husband. But seeing Tomiko so little changed, and judging too from the fact that at this hour he was still out on his rounds, leaving the estimate for the remodelling and all that up to his wife, Aki decided he must be a hard worker and a nice fellow but a timid, ineffectual sort of man.

Every time a train pulled in or out of the station, a minor tremor shook the room, but by the time they were drinking their after-dinner cup of tea, she didn't mind it so much.

"How are you? Any change since I saw you last?" Being suddenly questioned like this by Tomiko made Aki start. "Me?" she rejoined quizzically. "Oh, nothing in particular!" she said with a laugh, and then fell silent. Ever since she had first noticed Tomiko's smock, she had been thinking she must sooner or later broach the subject as casually as she could and ask about Tomiko's condition. Now's the time, she thought.

"Let's forget about me! What about you? When is it?" she asked in a low voice. Now, for a moment, it was Tomiko's turn to be taken aback, or so it appeared to Aki.

"If all goes according to schedule—January. No matter what, this time everything is going to be all right. My husband says so too."

The light had gone out of Tomiko's face. Her eyes had a fixed look about them. Aki searched for words to say, but no word she came up with seemed to be the right one; anything she said would only make matters worse!

"Look there!"

As she spoke, Tomiko pointed to a corner of the living room. When Aki had first been shown into the room, she had seen a corner heaped with flowers and just thought. There's the Buddha altar! But until they were now called to her attention, she had stupidly failed to notice the two small jars, standing low there side by side and all but buried under the flowers. The fetuses that had miscarried, as if this were determined by the waxing and the waning of the moon, and then the mourning rites that had to be gone through, as though it were all a matter of course. Tomiko talked about these things in a low voice, as if she were talking about someone else. She continued staring fixedly at the edge of the table while her fingertips groped for the chopsticks.

"But never mind! This time, you'll see! I'll have my baby properly!" And as she said this, Tomiko's eyes grew warm and smiling again.

But to Aki, it seemed as if she had suddenly been thrown into the middle of a thicket of prickly cactus, and no matter where she turned or how she looked about, she could see nothing like a path leading out of it. The overlapping fleshy leaves were slowly but deliberately swelling, getting fatter and fatter. The way they stretched upward, they seemed to be showing her how much they could grow. She felt a chill, as though convulsions had seized her body here and there; only her cheeks were burning.

On the way back from Tomiko's house, where a field of corn lay along the station railing, Aki vomited twice. She crouched there, steadying herself by holding on to several corn stalks bunched together, her back arched in misery like some stray cat that might have wandered that way. She had a vision of all those miscarried babies, clustered like so many grapes, gushing out over and over there before her eyes, feebly thrusting tiny hands and feet, rubbing up against each other, and after wriggling for a while, coming to rest quietly at last, in a white jar no bigger than a sake pourer.

Suddenly now, the end of her nightmare of a while ago comes back to Aki.

I seemed to be in a big room. Or maybe it wasn't that big after all. Pitch blackness all around, except for one single disc of light. I did not know what I was doing there, but as I stood there perfectly still, I thought, it's cold! Then that round brightness, which was the shining surface of some thick, dark solution, began to congeal with the cold and gave off a gleam that reminded me of blood. The surface of the liquid wavered. At first the gleam undulated gently. Then gradually the undulation changed into a great swell, and the liquid surface began to spread slowly. The liquid, fed from some unknown source, was surely increasing in volume, or so it appeared to me. In the interval between one swell and the next, some terribly soft-looking pinkish thing would rise up out of the top of the liquid and then sink back again, only to reappear from another part and sink back once more. Now the thick fluid was whirling and overflowing all around. I was going to be sucked into the maelstrom of that viscous gleam! Thinking only of how to escape from my rapidly mounting terror, I screamed "Quick!" as if urging someone to do something.

And then before I knew it, in a corner of the darkness, a pale face appeared, shining like a light. It did not immediately come close to me. I was at the limit of my endurance, but the rate of approach of that pale face was excruciatingly slow. I wanted to beckon to it, but my hand seemed to be pulled down by a great weight and I could not move it. When finally the face came close enough to see, I gave a start—

"Noboru!"

I do not know how many seconds later, how many hours later it was, but in the instant when his tenderness tried to reach out to me, I shivered all over and pushed him away.

Aki takes a resolute puff of her cigarette, then stubs it out in the ashtray. She switches off the bedside lamp. In the room below there is not a sound.

At this hour, when the cactuses and sago palms lift up their clustering limbs to the night sky, underneath the leaves the sleeping breath of animals will be wafted forth. The earth is white. The little spring is surely shining silver. Lazy but stubborn, that crowd of oh so very animal-like plants! A beating of the wings of unseen birds. A wild beast suddenly will rise from sleep and come crashing through the thicket and then violently shake itself, its eyes shining gold in the cool air of night.

Or again . . . in the heart of the city the buildings have at last recovered the coldness of the stone, while at the foundry, flames enwrap the furnace. The blistering cries of things that leave the womb and the gossamer-weak whimpers from the beds in the old people's home must melt and run together somewhere in the sky at night. Good fellowship and shame and boastfulness, the groans of the oppressed and long deep sighs like the receding tide; perhaps these also come together somewhere, whirling, whirling round and round. In the shade of all sorts of things are little sprouting lives making a secret gamble. But however secret the bet, however poor the chance, the thing that once begins to breathe alive will go on living in the dark night of the womb, deep in the amniotic sea, until the moon is full; untouched by doubt or hesitation, as if saying that the destiny laid down for it is simply this, to live.

Soon now, there will be a death that I must face. Aki is thinking of Setsuko, who must be asleep at this hour in her room at the university hospital. The day cannot be far off when all the malignancies spreading here and there through Setsuko's body, accompanied by unbearable pain, will plunge her senses into disorder. "The end has come," her doctor will say. With downcast eyes the nurse will cover her with a white starched sheet brought in from the laundry room, and they will gently carry her down to the morgue in the basement.

Just a week ago, I bought the eau de Cologne that Setsuko always uses and went and knocked lightly on the door of her sickroom. The woman attendant said "Please" as she showed me into the room, and went out looking happy to get away for a while. Setsuko's eyes were like two beads of glass that might have been set temporarily in the bone sockets. Her meagre flesh hung around her bones as if it were some sort of thick wrapping paper covering her temporarily. What I saw that day deep inside her were the thin burned-up bones; what I heard was the brittle crumbling of their white calcinated remains.

Setsuko's hospitalization had been decided on just half a year after her marriage. Then Setsuko's husband was appointed to a foreign post very shortly after. According to her, just like the diplomat her husband now accompanied, he himself was destined in the future to become a distinguished diplomat. From a café terrace that had a view of the Sphynx, from a brick-built city with rain-washed pavements, from the shores of a lake with a range of snow-clad mountains behind, he frequently sent her picture postcards. As soon as she recovered from this illness, he would come back and fetch her. "When that is done, next thing I will invite you to come and visit us. How many days can you get off from work?" And it seemed that Setsuko was making these plans in all seriousness.

Yes, but soon now Setsuko will be enveloped in rites of great solemnity. Summoned back from his foreign post, her husband will be reunited with his young wife in that dark room in the basement. His colleagues, Setsuko's friends, and the relatives on both sides will gather around Setsuko, now a corpse, and then soon they will hurry away again about their business. The husband will probably sit by Setsuko's side for a night. There will be the casket, the cremation, the solemn chanting of the sutras, the funeral flowers, the requiem music, the incense. Then he will take his wife in his arms, or all that's left of her—the calcinated bones and ashes—and he will leave, with all the other mourners following. In the deserted place of mourning there will be no sign of life until the garbageman appears, his hand towel round his head. He will come from the doorway and approach the altar and begin to clear away the funeral flower-wreaths.

There are caskets in hearses that glide gently forward, followed by the long chain of the funeral procession, and there are coffins dragged along on screeching pushcarts, tied down roughly with a common rope. There are people who gouge out the viscera of their dead and then wait upon the mountains for the birds, and there are people who scale precipices, their dead stuffed into leather bags upon their backs. There are secluded tombs away at the far end of well-kept avenues of approach flanked with statues of lions and of camels and of elephants, while by the shores of northern seas, are graves marked only by the native rocks forever lashed by stormy waves.

There are all kinds of rites to go with death.

In the royal palace there are rites that well befit the palaces of kings. Under roofs of tin are other rites more suited for a tin-roofed house. Sunlight, the stars, the trees, the honey in the flower, love . . . even lives that were snuffed out before they could know any of these things have their own special rites.

Aki has never seen Junko's dead body.

That big tilled field at twilight under great columns of cloud . . . that had become the backdrop for Aki's last memory of Junko in that place. With the orange-colored book she had taken from Aki's bookshelf under her arm, she had stopped in front of the farm-tool shed at the entrance to the field and said, "See you tomorrow." "'Bye! Say hello to your big sister for me, won't you!" Aki rejoined, to which Junko retorted, "And what about my big brother?" and then she stuck out her tongue. Their two laughing voices died away in the squeals of a child chasing dragonflies.

The little girl with the bucktoothed smile and hair in long plaits down her back never changed or grew an inch in Aki's mind from that time on. Even now, when the smell of hay comes to her, Aki will sometimes start. The pile of hay by the toolshed in that big tilled field was always hollowed by the weight of the two of them. On top of the hay Junko would go on and on talking about people she had never met as if they were acquaintances of long years' standing; even people who had been dead and buried for decades or even centuries, she would talk about in the same familiar way. And that is why, whenever she had to go off somewhere in connection with her work, if the wind happened to carry a whiff of new-mown hay through the window of the suburban train, Aki would find herself thinking that her relations with Junko, severed so many years before, were about to be resumed. With an upward glance she would scrutinize all the faces in the car she was riding in. But she never had any recollection of having seen a single one of those faces before. And yet, surely there was a smell of hay! Or was she just imagining things? And so, deciding she had been mistaken and trying to think of something else, she would lower her eyes again.

Aki has never seen Kiyoko's dead body.

Kiyoko had left Aki's house late that night. And that was the end of that. In the calm of the evening, the incessant croaking of the frogs intensified the impression of sultriness. After dinner, the two of them started on some beading work in Aki's room. They took turns going out on the veranda every time they heard a splash to chase away the night heron that stalked the carp in the garden pond. Then, while they were huddled together looking at some gold dust fallen from a large moth, Kiyoko promised to come to Aki's house again in two or three days' time. But that promise has yet to be kept. If Kiyoko were to walk into this room in a moment or two and stand there right in front of her, Aki would find nothing particularly strange or startling about that. It would merely be like a piece of movie film that had broken and was now patched together, restoring them to each other. "What happened? What have you been up to?" First of all they would look each other in the eye to make sure it was really the two of them, and then no doubt they'd grab and poke each other to make doubly sure, and everything would be all right again. Yes, thinks Aki, I am still waiting for Kiyoko!

Aki has never seen Kazue's dead body.

Nor Emiko's dead body.

No, nor Ikuko's.

Nor has she ever come across anyone else who witnessed their end or verified the deaths of Junko or Kiyoko or Kazue or Yayoi.

After that summer there were lots of people who for reasons of their own preferred to keep silent. Something must have happened to her friends to make them feel they didn't want Aki to see them. One of these days, surely, she'd meet Junko. Maybe she'll run into someone who has news of Kazue! And with these thoughts, Aki just went on waiting.

Sometimes the thought strikes Aki, maybe Junko is living right here in this same town without knowing that I am here too! Maybe she too is looking for me! Only, I am not in any of the places where she has looked. And she is not in any of the places where I have searched. Have we not perhaps gone on and on missing each other like that? Maybe in the train we have stood close together any number of times, back to back, and then got off and gone our separate ways. Maybe we have even sat in the same row at the theater, and then, unaware of each other's presence, left by different exits, one to the right, the other to the left. Maybe she was standing at the back of that elevator whose doors closed just as I was about to get on.

A year or so after that time, one day I ran into Yayoi's mother quite by chance, and she smiled and laughed at me, and not only at me but at all the people going by, and didn't seem the least bit embarrassed that she was in her bare feet. A few years later, the bloated corpse of Ikuko's younger sister was recovered from below the wharf where the logs are left to season in the water. The evening papers carried her picture and gave the cause of death as extreme nervous exhaustion. Tatsuo, who was to marry into Kazue's family in two or three years, because Kazue was missing, moved away and no longer lived in that place. An old established merchant family like that, and now, unless Kazue some day reappears, their line is doomed to die out.

In the devastated schoolground a mound of black earth had been raised and on top of it was just one plain wooden marker. Buried beneath in unglazed urns, indiscriminately gathered up with all those other deaths, must I recognize the deaths of Junko and Kiyoko and Kazue as well? Even so, if the dead, as they say, are never truly dead and will not rest in peace until the appropriate rites of mourning are performed for them, then the deaths of Junko and of Kiyoko and Kazue are not yet, so to speak, fully accomplished.

Now it is just three o'clock in the morning.

Aki gets up and opens the west window. She adjusts the collar of her robe and sits in the window, surveying the garden below. All the other lights in the building seem to be out, but the garden lamp casts a round of glimmering brightness on the ground. At the center of this circle of light is a small potting shovel that someone threw aside. A tricycle sits astride the line of the circumference.

Still from time to time the lightning streaks in its erratic course across the night sky. After its light goes out, the trees and houses seem to plunge into an even deeper blackness.

Spreading beyond the edge of the garden is a vegetable field. If you cross that you come to the riverbeach. Since we've had no rain for some time, the water level will have dropped. Maybe you can even see the pebbles in the riverbed. Where the weir has dammed the water up, will the river fish be sleeping soundly?

Last evening, for the first time in days, there was a beautiful sunset. Intending to go to the public bath, she began to put her toilet things together. Then with her washbasin under her arm, Aki leaned out of the window.

"Hands up!"

The block of apartments had a bend in the middle like a hook: from the downstairs apartment diagonally opposite, two little boys, brothers, barefoot and dressed only in swimming trunks, came dashing out together. Then, as if they had planned it in advance, they suddenly darted apart, one to the right, the other to the left, and from behind the trunks of the garden's few trees they started shooting at each other. Bang, Baannng! Bang, Baannng!

The young mother began scolding from inside the apartment. "What's happened to your shoes? And your caps?"

After a little bout of gunning, the boys raced into the house again, still making shooting noises. As they ran in, they met a girl in a yellow dress coming out. She emptied the water out of a bucket with a boat floating in it and collected the sneakers they had trampled and knocked every which way, and as she went around tidying everything up, she turned and shouted to the inside of the house, "Uncle will be home early today, won't he, Auntie?"

Because it is Saturday, of course. Soon now, "Uncle" will be honking the horn of his Publica and the boys will go dashing out, yelling, "Papa's home!" And the two will start tugging at the coattails of their father who will be carrying a box of pastries for dessert and rattling his car keys as he comes. They will grab at the keys. Aki can see it all as if it were already happening before her eyes. The window pane of the apartment the boys ran into now has six palms spread against it like so many pressed flowers.

All of a sudden everything went quiet. The stillness was so deep it made you wonder that even a block of apartments like this one could experience such an hour. Aki looked slowly about the place. A watering can abandoned in the sandbox; a plastic pool, blobs of sand on the bottom looking like a map; a patch of dried plaster; under the eaves a lizard that seemed as if it had been pasted on; a clothes line already gone slack; trees bent low as if their own weight had been too much for them to bear; a bucket only half full, left behind in the common laundry area; the rubbish dump with papers sticking out of it; an improvised garage that looked more like a box for toys . . . the sound of the cicadas, penetrating as a brush stroke on paper, had now died away.

Aki put the washbasin she had been holding on the table and then, leaning against the window frame, inhaled her cigarette. She blew the first puff of smoke straight at the middle of the sky. Just then, the western sky was one great blaze of splendor.

Yes, straight over there, at the far edge of the vegetable field that stretches out beyond the block of apartments, yesterday's setting sun went right down the chimney of that brick house. It was majestic, solemn. Moment by moment the colors changed; it was like watching scenery in a series of hurriedly shifted slides. A quiet peaceful Saturday. It was indeed a fitting end to a fine summer's day.

But at the close of that other summer's day, the bright evening glow was not caused simply by the setting sun. The blue first faded from the eastern sky and gradually it sank into black ink, but though the darkness grew and deepened, the evening glow was not the least bit dimmed. On the contrary, as the other side of the sky darkened, it burned all the more brightly, and seemed to be spreading and spreading. Aki crouched low in a hollow in a field with people she had never seen before that day, and stared steadily up at that night sky.

The morning, the great flash, the big bang, the squall of wind, the fire . . . all these I can remember very clearly, but what happened to me next? That was a blank in her memory that Aki was not able to fill in.

When she recovered her senses she found herself running in the direction of the sea, borne along in a rush of total strangers. Shirts in shreds, scorched trousers, bloodsoaked blouses, yukatas with a sleeve missing, seared and blistered skin, an old man just sitting there watching the people rush by before his eyes, a woman with a child in each arm, a barefoot university student, someone screaming, "The fire is coming!" When she looked back at the town it was engulfed in black smoke. As for what was happening inside it, at the time Aki had no idea, and even to think of it was too horrifying.

Why did she have this thing with her? Aki was crouching in the hollow she had managed to struggle to, an empty bucket in front of her. The eyes of the people gathered there were abnormally bright and their voices strangely high-pitched. Whenever there was a moment's lull in the noise and confusion, the low roar of the sea could be heard. As evening wore on, the crowd of grotesque figures in the hollow continued to grow.

It was already the hour of the afterglow, but the sky was blazing with the excess of heat from the earth, and all through the night it continued to burn a fiery red, until at last, in the brightness slowly spreading from the east, it lost its incandescent glow. Up to daybreak, ominous noises like an avalanche shook the hollow several times. When the wind shifted, it carried a reek of burning fat. Now and then, a frog croaked somewhere.

Aki longed for the morning. With morning everything would be better. If she could just make it through this night, things would be all right. That was the feeling that sustained her.

Ah, but that morning, so breathlessly awaited it had hurt, what did it have to show to Aki? Things that for so long she had seen with her own eyes and touched with her own hands, and whose existence she had never even thought to doubt, taking their being there so much for granted, she now could find no more, except in some far corner of her memory, deep in her consciousness. With her lips slightly parted, Aki stood transfixed with horror. Broken stumps of old trees were still smouldering. Molten metal ran along the pavement. A great geyser gushed out where the lid of the water main had exploded. All around as far as eye could see, nothing but ruin and rubble, and strewn on top of all, as if left behind there by mistake, strange objects of some whitish chalky substance.

The far-off hills, in some strange way, seemed to be closing in upon the town.

It is not an act of Heaven.

It is not an act of Earth.

No! It can't be that!

But at the time, Aki had not an inkling of the real nature of this thing that set her knees knocking together in sheer terror.

And Aki, standing petrified there, now became aware of an eery stillness that seemed to be about to envelop her body. Presently it wrapped her round with a gentleness she had never known or felt before. Perhaps I am going to be shut in for all eternity somewhere at the bottom of the earth, she thought. It was not long before she felt herself being sucked down into a black abyss. Innumerable little yellow arrows flew before her eyes, bewildering her, and she felt herself falling, falling down into a blank that had cut off the light. There was no longer anything left of the great gentleness. Aki was now being manipulated by something hard and resistant. Something was over; she could not but think that. Rather than question the existence of the thing that now sought to gain control of her, she merely felt the pity of it all.

Suddenly, something white jumped out of the rubbish dump and streaked across the garden in a straight line, making for the vegetable field beyond. A cat, most likely. As if suddenly remembering to do so, the wind now shook the branches of the trees.

It was not quite true for Aki to say that she had never experienced before that summer's day the feeling of being all at once enveloped in an eery stillness and then falling, falling down into the blank that cut the light off. Why? Because although dim and far away, she now suddenly remembered a night long ago, when she had felt herself slip all at once into a black abyss, a night she now was dredging up from the immeasurable depths of her subconscious.

"Good night! Now go to sleep!" the nurse said, moving away from Aki's side. After looking at the thermometer hung on a post, she left the room. Aki stretched herself under the quilt. She was full of that feeling of well-being that comes when a high temperature returns to normal. Tonight too, no doubt, there will be lots of guests. Father and mother, but especially mother, will be tired out attending to them. The maid too will be busily bustling about. From the main house on the other side of the patio came the clatter of a late dinner. In the moonlight, the dwarfed pine lifted its twisted trunk, and the white sand spread around it in the pot gleamed silvery white.

When all the shutters were put up in the main house, she felt how isolated was the little detached room where she now slept.

How much time had passed she did not know, but after a while Aki thought she heard voices outside the earthen wall. They stopped for a while and then went on again in low tones. They were voices she did not remember ever having heard before. They were certainly not the voices of the gatekeeper and his wife. Because a stream from the hill had been diverted through their garden, sometimes people coming down the hill strayed in by mistake. Maybe the voices of a while ago belonged to some people like that. But no matter how much time went by, there was no change in the location of the voices. After a while, they began to grow gradually louder. There was a man's voice, low but somehow angry. At long intervals the thin voice of a woman mingled with it. The hard-to-catch voice of the man grew louder and rougher. The woman's voice presently changed to a low convulsive sobbing. Then there was a dull thump, as though part of one body had struck a terrible blow at a part of the other body. Aki instinctively hid her head under the quilt. She had heard what she was not supposed to hear, hadn't she? A ringing started deep within her ears. She had a strange feeling of being shot at with countless yellow arrows, all coming straight at her.

Why was she upsetting herself over that unknown woman who was undoubtedly cowering on the other side of the garden wall? Aki, still only a child, did not know, but in some obscure hurt way she felt a sense of identity with the woman beyond the wall. Are all women doomed to weep like that when they grow up? Even women whose tears I have never once seen; for example, that nurse so attentive and good with sick people and apparently trusted by the doctor, or the teacher of my elementary school class who stands on her platform every day looking as if she never gave a thought to anything but the government textbooks: do women like that too, late in the night, go someplace we don't know and cry their hearts out there in floods of tears? Aki felt that she was falling, falling down into a black abyss, and then discovered that she herself was crying.

The day of her visit to Tomiko, just as they were settling down with the table between them, Tomiko had looked Aki in the eye and asked, "When did you last go back home?"

The place where Tomiko was born and which she calls her home she seems to think is naturally "home" for Aki too. But when Tomiko questioned her like that, Aki found she could not answer right away. As she looked at Tomiko, it seemed that already the words were breaking into fragments in her head, GO—BA—CK—HO—ME.

Since we two had not seen each other for four or five years, it was not inappropriate for Tomiko to start talking about that place, thought Aki. It's not just Tomiko. Lots of other people, either by way of greeting or because they really want to know how things are now in that place, ask me the same question. They probably don't mean anything by it. But that place where Tomiko and I were born and raised and from which the fire drove us out—is that a proper place for me to go back to, just like that, as Tomiko says, without the slightest hesitation? What exactly in that place would I be going home to? If there is something there that's fitting to return to, I want it to be a something that endures unchanged and transcends time. Something of which it may be said, now *that* at least is certain. People should return to something that, no matter what may happen, will endure and still be seen as the true root and source of what they are.

When the night of the Bon Lantern Festival came around, Tomiko and I would often go down to the pier together. On several occasions we got on the same boat. "Mr. Boatman, please row out that way; no! further out into the offing," and the two of us side by side at the gunwale would watch the other boats pass by. "Ah! that one was the Masudaya's boat, and the one coming from over there is surely the Sasaya's boat!" And chattering away like that, we would stay on until quite late, blown by the night winds. Scattered over the waters, then brushing against each other again, those lanterns for the departed souls were as vivid in Aki's mind as something she might have seen just now on the riverbeach beyond the vegetable field.

Does Tomiko still remember? The thin little bones, the pale pink insides of the nearly transparent fish in their shoals? The wharf bridge darkening the water below? The five-colored pinwheels stuck between the cotton candy stall and the white mice cages, and that resonance of expectancy along the shrine path at the time of the clan god's festival? The window full of the Milky Way, and when you opened it that smell of oil from the armory that nearly knocked you out? The castle tower, the parade ground, the napes of the young men's necks, the henhouse, the greenhouse, the shipyard, the schoolhouse, the warehouse, the heat shimmer, the carrying chest, the armor case . . . ?

The old men, gathered under the ornamental light that looked like a sea anemone, would soon be deep in talk. Hiding behind her back, I would slip in with the maid who went to serve them their black tea. The first of them to spot me would beckon with his hand and say, "Aki, there's a good little girl, come over here to grandpa!"

The wallpaper was pretty well faded but you could still clearly make out the picture pattern. The Pyramids towered in the distance. A woman was washing a jar in the stream. The animals seemed to be asleep in the shade of the trees while a man sat nearby. The old men talked on and on as if they were never going to stop. "Salt-broiling is the only thing for *ayu* trout, eh!" "What's happened to all the women?" "Now the difference between the treeleaf butterfly of the Ryūkyūs and the treeleaf butterfly of Taiwan is this . . . ."

That time when, in the bright sunshine, I gazed on the vast multitude of dead in all the chaos of that ruined ground, laid waste and desolate by someone or by something yet unknown, with my knees knocking together out of control, the thing I kept telling myself was this: it is only a temporary phenomenon! I kept on pursuing the original appearance of that place as it had been before, and as I was sure it would be again. Maybe tomorrow I will see Junko! Maybe I'll come across someone who knows how Kiyoko is! When I was trying to sleep out under the starry sky with such thoughts in my mind, the awareness that began to seep through the depths of my consciousness, the thing I took to thinking as if it were most natural was this: Junko and Kiyoko, sometime, somewhere, will surely appear before me once again!

At that time, what on earth did I consider the original appearance of that place? Was it the limpid flowing stream, so clear that you could see the pebbles in the riverbed? Was it the trees along the roads with their load of soft green buds? Was it the tilled field where the earth was neither hard nor black nor dry when turned over? Was it the harmony that prevailed among all these? Or was it the dawn city when the fish peddlers went by? The sound of rackets batting the ball back and forth until near twilight on the schoolyard tennis court? The white walled castle? But all these, alas, are things doomed to change, now no longer fit to bear the weight of changelessness! I felt I had been witness on that morning to a temporary phenomenon that later, sometime, must be overcome and gone beyond. But perhaps I was wrong. The term temporary phenomenon should not have referred only to the scene of devastation; it should have covered, too, the great flash, the big bang, the squall of wind, and it should perhaps also have included that place that dawned and darkened to the low roar of the sea. It struck me then that something certainly had ended there. I was perhaps one of the witnesses to the end of a particular phenomenon.

But that thought too may have been wrong. Its present condition, its broad paved streets, its tall buildings, its airport, its foreign cars, its stadium, its cinemas, its bars . . . all those things are enough to make one doubt the reality of what once happened in that place. From now on, too, new schools will be put up. More and more trees will line the city's streets. There will be more and more roller coasters in more amusement parks. But there are times, nevertheless, when I am struck with the dread premonition that suddenly one day all those tall buildings will come tumbling down. I have visions of the pavements splitting open, of the foreign cars abandoned in the streets and turned to lumps of burnt-down metal. They will be like these other things in the world of my memory, that in a twinkling were all changed and lost. And this is true not only of that place as it is now. All these familiar things about me every day, this table, this bookshelf, this mirror, this clock, these people boxed into their several compartments, and—standing here and holding all of that—this block of apartments, the street lights, the suspension bridge, the superhighway, the lockers in the drafting room, the bones of kindly gentle people. It seems to me I hear the sound of all these things crumbling down. And I myself am nothing more than another of these things doomed to crumble! Aki thinks of her own self, her body blown to bits, reduced to chalky handfuls left exposed to every wind. But, just like life, is not death, too, simply one of the many faces of existence?

Even if it has only a tin roof I don't mind! I want to sleep somewhere that isn't out on the bare ground!

I don't mind if it isn't in a glass! I want some clean water that you're not afraid to drink!

Even a piece so small it fits into the hollow of my hand, I don't mind! I want to see myself in something you could call a mirror!

Even if it's that mean, nasty Taeko, I don't mind! I want to talk to someone that is not a grown-up stranger wrapped in bandages!

But several nights were to pass in the hollow before even a single one of these simple wishes of Aki's would come true.

The great anger, the deep hate, come after the event. The thing that parted me from Junko, that kept Kiyoko from me although she wanted to see me again, that made me cower all night in a hollow in the ground—if I could catch the real nature of that thing and fling the fullness of my anger and hate at it, I would not be in torment to this day, well over ten years after, tied to this fierce anger that still finds no proper outlet. I would not be tortured by this nameless hate that yet finds no clear object. This is what Aki thinks.

Sometimes Aki, on her way to the office in the morning, would suddenly think she had found it, would see that object clearly. At the midday break, opening the window of the drafting room and looking up at a cloudless sky, there were times she felt she saw it float up quite clearly, with no further need for doubt. I must not let this out of my sight! Now, how can I get my anger and indignation across to this, their object? Aki would begin to lay her plan with meticulous care. But as she pursued that object, its contours would grow vague, and then some other object more or less linked with it would intrude. The new object was always inevitably linked with the old. One after another new objects would appear and then grow vague and blurred. And a further trouble: Aki began to suspect uneasily that the hazy something that had lost its clear outlines might be her own self.

I am ashamed to say I still cannot see where I had best direct my hate and anger, but . . . and Aki went on thinking. The rite that should have been performed and never was, and my unassuaged thirst for it, I must recognize as the beginning of a questioning of "being" that I must now develop. Wherein lies the realness of things? Can you say that a thing that's really there and that you can be sure of is one your eyes can see, your hands can touch, your skin can feel? The things in your consciousness, that you can neither see nor touch, are they less truly there?

But what degree of realness is there in things your eyes can see, your hands can touch, or your skin can feel? Setsuko's husband was not by her side in that sickroom. But when Setsuko looked up at the map of the world pasted on the wall beside her bed and thought about her husband in his foreign post, was he not truly there within her mind? Surely then he was a more weighty presence in her consciousness than when he was beside her, touching her, and she would waken with a sense that he was slipping far away from her like a draft of wind. And can the senses grasp reality as well as she could with her consciousness, once she could cease to treat as an unreal thing the presence in it?

"What do you think of it? Those people starting out simultaneously from the far ends of the Silk Road to meet in the middle?"

Noboru put this question to Aki as they were having dinner in a restaurant that overlooked the nighttime sea. With a vivacity unusual for him, his eyes slightly clouded from the little whiskey he had drunk, he kept on talking to Aki of one thing after another. He seemed to have a compulsion to talk. He even felt impelled to speak to the waiter who came to clear the table, saying such things as "The butter sauce with the fish-meunière is very good here" or "This coffee must be a blend of at least three varieties of beans." There were not many customers. The air conditioning in the room was too cold for Aki in her short sleeved blouse.

After dinner, Aki walked along the shore road with Noboru. As they walked, Aki, comforted by Noboru, had her spirits restored but saw it all as too late. I want to go on walking for a long, long time, she thought. But that same evening, when Noboru had reduced to nothing the distance that separated them, Aki found herself caught up in the eery stillness. Feeling as if someone else had suddenly come up behind and laid a hand on her shoulder to pull her back, she shuddered. She said, "Any moment now, I am going to fall into that black abyss!" And then Noboru, anguish showing in his face, muttered in a low voice, "I know; but you must forget all about that kind of thing. If you really loved me, you would be able to put that sort of thing right out of your mind!"

What Aki, in the grip of that eery stillness, foresaw in dire premonition was Noboru, blind still himself to all the signs, Noboru hideously changed beyond all recognition, as Aki herself must change! In the taxi on the way back, the two of them hardly opened their mouths. Noboru looked out the window. In his rear view mirror, the driver kept darting quizzical glances at the back seat.

Aki lit a fresh cigarette.
After that I didn't meet him for quite a while, not until the winter. On that bookshelf there will be several books lent to me by Noboru. "If you want to study the houses of Granada, this one is good. If you are more interested in Madrid, this one here is best." It seems to her she can hear his voice.
I still had his books and I should have returned them to him when I saw him for the last time in the winter, yet I failed to do so! There is someting wrong with me . . . .

Rejected, Noboru's slightly twisted face drew slowly back. Aki had felt the reproach in his eyes as she turned her cheek away. Gently she loosened his arm. The utter wretchedness of letting go of warmth and tenderness went right through her. Her voice was very low and small when she said, "I'm sorry," and it was swallowed up immediately in the dark sea before her eyes. The risen tide was beating steadily against the breakwater. The invisible thread that had drawn Noboru and herself together had now snapped, thought Aki, while another Aki whispered to her, "But it is you yourself, isn't it, who let go of the thread! It is you yourself, isn't it, who refuse to see him any more! You're a fool, that's what you are! Maybe so, but . . . . "
It was snowing.
Far out a ship's siren wailed.
Aki, who had lowered her gaze to the water's surface, now

raised it gradually and then turned her whole face up. The snow was not coming from any very high place, but rather seemed to be gushing quietly out and falling softly down from somewhere quite near.

Noboru must think I didn't really love him. But I don't have the strength to go on explaining about that dread awareness that suddenly took hold of me.

Aki bit her lip. The snow was falling cold on her cheeks. Only the backs of her eyes were scalding hot. She could feel his gaze on her from behind, so piercing that it hurt, as she said "Let's go!" Taking the lead, she set off walking ahead of him. Naturally, he must have been terribly hurt and have taken this to mean that his love was not returned. Children hooded against the cold were running about the deck of one of the boats at anchor in the canal. On the deck of another, a number of young sailors were warming themselves around a fire they had made in an oil drum. They spotted Noboru and Aki and their individual spontaneous whistles came together in a chorus. That was the end of the year before last.

It is a little after four in the morning.

That small light beyond the vegetable garden—is it from the brick house? Or maybe it's some nearer light. The trees and houses are still plunged in darkness. Aki automatically smooths her front hair with the palm of her left hand. Her eyes pick out a tree. When I think of Noboru, quite often I remember at the same time that night so long ago when I broke down and cried for an unknown woman. Of all past nights, why do I have to pick out that one? Or is it perhaps that I am trying to relive it in the unconscious? All that is very vague. The two things seem to be totally unconnected, yet in some obscure way you can also see that they are profoundly linked. But that summer when I witnessed in that place the sudden loss of all I thought was mine and the omission of the rite that should have been performed, something that lay dormant until then suddenly colored me, and its dye deepened rapidly. I think I can say that. Now, on the contrary, that thing is trying to gain control of me, and I am questioning anew the meaning of existence. What we call dying, what we call living, things that are or that are not—what exactly are all these things? No doubt I'll go on groping, questioning, bearing the burden of this anger that I cannot vent, and this hate that still finds no clear object. I want to live without wiping out the memory of that day! My ancestors were slaves in Egypt . . . like the people of Israel, who at the Feast of the Passover, yearning to break free from bondage, woke from sleep and resumed reading their dark records. At that time, their thoughts probably ran like this—Someone who can just casually wipe out the memory of his own history will not be fit, as history unfolds, to play the role of a great hero.

That place of mine that was so beautiful—if it was truly mine, then that same place when hideously changed by someone or some force unknown to me was surely also mine. To the question of which is really the true place, I cannot answer now with any confidence. If one speaks in terms of a phenomenon, then both were that. If asked which was reality, I am inclined to say that both were also that. But surely what I called unchanging, the abiding source one can always go home to, must be something richer far than either, rejecting neither of them but transcending both. It must be something solidly sustained by an imperturbable order, although it may reveal itself under the varying aspects of separate phenomena. Yes, I shall no doubt go to that place again, but I will not be going home. What makes me think so is that host of things lost to my sight, no more reliable than fluff or down, and the uncertainty of all the things I see before me every day. To my regret, that imperturbable order is now known to me only within the world of wishful intimations. But I must know if it really exists. If I could know it, even in a flash of intuition, then perhaps I would no longer be the prey of this eery stillness that takes hold of me. I would be freed then from my terror of being sucked into that void that blocks out the light and of falling down, down, down into that black abyss. I want to know.

Slowly, softly now, a whiteness starts to spread, beneath a sky that seems to be melting quietly away, and the shapes of trees and houses at last stand out. A thick mist will be creeping along the river, brushing the wings of the still sleeping crane flies on the dewy grasses of the riverbeach. Any moment now, the alarm bell at the grade crossing will start ringing. Soon the garden swing will be encircled by the joyous shrieks of children. A man still in his night clothes will cut through the squeals of delight with a yell of "Breakfast!" A woman will come out to fetch them, and the children, with a hand in each of hers, will disappear again inside the door. A deliveryman will appear beyond the shrubbery. A bill collector, taking advantage of the holiday with everyone at home, will be approaching from beyond the rubbish heap. In the makeshift garage, the engine of the Publica will soon be starting up. "'Bye! See you later! Have a nice holiday!"

Soon the night will be over. Let me get some sleep! And Aki draws the window curtain shut.

translated by Eileen Kato

About the Authors

Introduction by Kenzaburō Ōe

Kenzaburō Ōe (January, 1935—   ) was born in Ehime Prefecture. The publication of "Kimyō na Shigoto" ["A Strange Job"] in 1957, while Ōe was still a student in the French literature department of Tokyo University, marked the beginning of his literary career. In 1958, he was awarded the Akutagawa Prize for "The Catch." His first full-length novel *Me mushiri Ko uchi* [*Plucking Buds and Shooting Lambs*], published in the same year, also won great acclaim. He received his degree from Tokyo University in 1959, his graduation thesis being on Sartre. Notable among his works are *Warera no Jidai* [*Our Time*] (1959), *A Personal Matter* (1964), a documentary entitled *Hiroshima Notes* (1964–65), *Ōe Kenzaburō Zenshū* [*The Complete Works of Ōe Kenzaburō*] (1966–67), and a collection of lectures entitled *Kakujidai no Sōzōryoku* [*Imagination in the Atomic Age*] (1970). His most recent novel *Rouse Up, O Young Men of the New Age!* was published in 1983, and he continues to maintain his position as a front-runner in the contemporary literary scene.

The Crazy Iris by Masuji Ibuse

Masuji Ibuse (February, 1898—   ) was born in Hiroshima and attended the French literature department of Waseda University. He appeared on the literary scene with the publication of "Salamander" in 1929, and thereafter continued to write in a style characterized by a unique blend of humor and bitterness. He was awarded the Naoki Prize for *John Manjiro, the Cast-Away; His Life and Adventure* and has continued to publish works filled with warmth and kindliness, while at the same time showing his keen powers of observation. In 1966, he was awarded the Order of Cultural Merit for *Black Rain*, which describes the tragedy of Hiroshima with a calm restraint. John Bester's English translation of *Black Rain* was published by Kodansha International in 1969. "The Crazy Iris" was first published in 1951.

Summer Flower / The Land of Heart's Desire by Tamiki Hara

Tamiki Hara (November, 1905—March, 1951) was born in Hiroshima. While he was a middle school student, he became familiar with Russian literature, and also began to write poetry. He particularly admired the poets Saisei Murō and Paul Verlaine. He graduated from the English literature department of Keiō University, and was later exposed to the atomic bomb in Hiroshima. This terrifying experience produced stories such as "Summer Flower," for which he was awarded the first Takitarō Minakami Prize, and "Chinkon Ka" ["Requiem"], which are now considered to be among his finest works. He committed suicide in 1951. "Summer Flower" was first published in 1947, and "The Land of Heart's Desire" in 1951.

Human Ashes by Katsuzō Oda

Katsuzō Oda (November, 1931—   ) was born in Osaka and attended the English literature department of Waseda University. He was exposed to the atomic bomb while working as a student recruit. In 1966, he published "Human Ashes" in the magazine «Yūsei», the organ of the Ministry of Posts and Telecommunications, and was awarded the magazine's 8th literary prize. Through the recommendations of Jun Etō and Shūsaku Endō, who had served as judges for «Yūsei», he began to publish stories in «Gunzō», a popular literary magazine. His cool, detached narrative style cloaks the horror of his experiences as an atomic bomb victim, enabling him to maintain an aesthetic balance. "Human Ashes" was republished in a well-known literary magazine in 1969.

Fireflies by Yōko Ōta

Yōko Ōta (November, 1906—December, 1963) was born in Hiroshima. As a young girl she read Takuboku Ishikawa and Shūsei Tokuda, as well as Goethe and Heine. She also read and was influenced by Tolstoi. On the invitation of Kan Kikuchi, she came to Tokyo, where she began to work as a magazine reporter. She worked her way into the literary scene through her involvement in the activities of several literary magazines. In 1940, Sakura no Kuni [The Cherry Land] was awarded a prize by the «Asahi» newspaper, and received considerable public acclaim. Miss Ōta was exposed to the atomic bomb in Hiroshima. Stricken with the fear that she would become a victim of radiation sickness, she worked feverishly to complete *Shikabane no Machi* [*The City of Corpses*], an account of her experiences in Hiroshima at the time of the bombing. *Ningen Ranru* [*Human Shabbiness*] was awarded the Women's Literature Prize. "Fireflies" was first published in 1953.

The Colorless Paintings by Ineko Sata

Ineko Sata (June, 1904—   ) was born in Nagasaki. After graduating from elementary school, she moved with her family to Tokyo. The family was poor, and Ineko worked at various jobs as a young girl. When she was 22, she met Tatsuo Hori and Shigeharu Nakano and became a member of the staff of the literary magazine «*Roba*», in which her maiden work "Kyarameru Kōjō kara" ["From the Caramel Factory"] was published. She later participated in the proletarian literature movement, and was arrested and imprisoned many times. She has continued to publish works such as *Onna no Yado* [*A Lodge for Women*] (1963), and *Juei* [*The Shadow of Trees*] (1972), both of which were awarded literary prizes, and which show her sincerity as a revolutionary writer and as a woman. "The Colorless Paintings" was first published in 1961.

The Empty Can by Kyōko Hayashi

Kyōko Hayashi (August, 1930—   ) was born in Nagasaki and spent the years from 1931 to 1945 in Shanghai. After returning to Japan, she was enrolled in the third year of Nagasaki Girls' High School and was exposed to the atomic bomb while working as a recruit in the Mitsubishi Munitions Factory. She later studied for a time in a special course for women affiliated with the Nagasaki Medical University. "Ritual of Death" in which she described her experiences as an atomic bomb victim with a restrained lyricism, was awarded the 73rd Akutagawa Prize. "The Empty Can" was first published in 1978.

The House of Hands by Mitsuharu Inoue

Mitsuharu Inoue (May, 1926—   ) was born in Lüshun (Port Arthur), China. After World War II, he joined the Communist Party of Japan. In 1950 he published "Kakarezaru Isshō" ["The

Chapter that Must be Written"], in which he attacked the corruption within the party, and left the party in 1953. In 1963 he published *Chi no Mure* [*People of the Land*], which inquires into the way people live in post-war Japan, focusing on victims of the atomic bomb, and in 1966, *Kuroi Shinrin* [*The Black Forest*], which criticizes Stalinism. He has since continued to produce fine works which capture the tension of post-war Japan in a unique and distinguished style. In 1970, he began to edit his own quarterly magazine «*Henkyō*». "The House of Hands" was first published in 1960.

The Rite by Hiroko Takenishi

Hiroko Takenishi (April, 1929—   ) was born in Hiroshima. After graduating from the Japanese literature department of Waseda University, she worked for two major publishing companies, but left her job in 1962. She began to publish critical essays in a private literary magazine, and in 1964 was awarded a literary prize for a collection of critical essays on classical Japanese literature. She has gained recognition as an unusual critic whose mind moves back and forth between the classics and modern literature. In 1978 she was awarded the Women's Literature Prize for "Kan Gen Sai" ["The Orchestra Festival"], which links the atomic bomb to the present. "The Rite" was first published in 1963.

THE ORIGINAL TITLES

Toward the Unknowable Future   Kenzaburō Ōe
何とも知れない未来に   大江健三郎

The Crazy Iris   Masuji Ibuse
かきつばた   井伏鱒二

Summer Flower   Tamiki Hara
夏の花   原　民喜

The Land of Heart's Desire   Tamiki Hara
心願の国   原　民喜

Human Ashes   Katsuzō Oda
人間の灰   小田勝造

Fireflies   Yōko Ōta
ほたる   大田洋子

The Colorless Paintings   Ineko Sata
色のない画   佐多稲子

The Empty Can   Kyōko Hayashi
空罐   林　京子

The House of Hands   Mitsuharu Inoue
手の家   井上光晴

The Rite   Hiroko Takenishi
儀式   竹西寛子